THE GODS
OF CERUS MAJOR

THE GODS
OF CERUS MAJOR

GARY ALAN RUSE

DOUBLEDAY & COMPANY, INC.

GARDEN CITY, NEW YORK

1982

All of the characters in this book
are fictitious, and any resemblance
to actual persons, living or dead,
is purely coincidental.

Library of Congress Cataloging in Publication Data

Ruse, Gary Alan, 1946–
The gods of Cerus Major.

(Doubleday science fiction)
I. Title. II. Series.
PS3568.U72G6   813'.54
AACR2
ISBN 0-385-17118-8
Library of Congress Catalog Card Number 80–2626

First Edition

For all my dear friends at the FAU Conference on the Fantastic!

CONTENTS

THE GODS
OF CERUS MAJOR

CHAPTER 1

THE *ECLIPSE*

"Gentlemen, prepare for space leap," Jason Smith ordered. The young commander of the massive space cruiser *Eclipse* watched as the members of his crew hurried to take their places at various points around the operations deck of the vessel. All except one man, who was not a crew member at all, but a passenger.

Oleg Rondell, the stout government representative who had bullied his way out of the passenger compartment for a privileged seat on the operations deck, continued studying the indicators on the equipment consoles with aloof curiosity, bending over a lighted display here and a control device there, seemingly oblivious to Jason's order. His abrasive manner and endless questions about the newly developed space-leap systems had certainly not endeared him to the crew members, and now he was beginning to get on Jason's nerves as well.

"That order applies to *diplomats* as well as gentlemen," Jason told him pointedly. "Surely, Representative, we must have at least one nonacceleration niche that is adequate for a man of your . . . stature."

Rondell looked up abruptly, flashing Jason a disdainful smirk. He located the nearest nonacceleration niche between two banks of equipment and squeezed his rotund form into the space. The modular gel lining compressed around him, adjusted to his shape and held him safely immobile.

"Satisfied, Commander?" Rondell's polite words were dripping with sarcasm.

Jason ignored him. Turning to Brant, the *Eclipse*'s flight engineer, he said, "Open main power circuits one and two. We won't need maximum output for a test."

"Right, sir." Brant quickly worked the controls, activating the electromagnetic fields deep within the ship, channeling the stored energy from the primary chambers into the propulsion system.

Jason leaned back in the gel-lined commander's chair and studied the Tri-D view dome in the center of the forward wall. The great concave screen presently showed a 180-degree forward view of space, but the image could be shifted to show the reverse direction as well.

In the center of the screen, marked by a pulsating pattern of lights, was Space Port One, giant docking platform orbiting the Earth. Even at their present distance the platform looked immense, as indeed it was. The massive framework of docks, control pods and connecting ways was one third the diameter of the moon. The *Eclipse* itself had been constructed there, and was essentially a modified cargo vessel refitted to accept the new propulsion system.

"Test coordinates laid in, sir." The words had come from Danfield Clark, the ship's British-born first officer. "Everything's secure."

"Let's get it done, then." Jason turned to Brant at the flight controls. "Activate the system."

"Beginning now, sir."

A pulsing throb began as the trans-space generators built up power. In his niche, Rondell braced himself for the attendant jolt he had been told to expect. The precaution was unnecessary, however, since the gel lining would absorb virtually all of the impact. He almost regretted that the lot had fallen to him for the mission to Betalon, but knew it was essential if he hoped to advance his career in the diplomatic service. So far he had only been sent to the near worlds, and he would never achieve high status if he held back now. He only hoped they had gotten all of the bugs out of the new transport system.

"Achieving leap power now, sir," Clark called out.

The throb became a muffled whine that reverberated throughout the great spherical space cruiser. Sitting motionless in space like a small metallic moon, the cruiser's hull began to display a shift in color. The intensity of reflected light from its shiny silver surface diminished, and in another moment the craft had become completely invisible.

Inside, Oleg Rondell watched in bewildered appreciation. The lines of the operations deck became hazy and indistinct. The crew members looked like transparent blue ghosts. Rondell was glad that he could not look down and see his own body.

Then the jolt.

It was a distinct snap that seemed to pluck at the mind as well as the physical body. For a brief instant a feeling of incredible energies and movement. Then, in as brief an instant, a complete cessation of the energies—a null, a vast empty feeling, slightly unpleasant. It did not last long.

"Energy field stabilizing," Clark reported in his precise British tone. "We've made the jump."

Jason Smith leaned forward in his chair. The view dome displayed a slightly altered image.

The Earth was now but a tiny glowing dot in the vastness of space. Space Port One was a tinier dot, barely visible near the horizon of the distant planet. The remainder of the image was seemingly unchanged, owing to the infinitely greater distance to even the nearest star.

"What's our position?" Jason said.

"Just beyond the orbit of Mars," Clark responded. "Precisely on the coordinates I laid in. The system's functioning flawlessly."

"So far. But that was only a minimal leap. The distance to Betalon is a million times greater." Jason glanced toward the niche which held Oleg Rondell. The diplomat had worked both hands free of the gel lining and was probing his face and torso with tentative fingers, as if to reassure himself that his body was once again a material thing with substance. Jason could not suppress a grin. "Feeling all right, Representative?"

"What—?" Rondell looked up with sudden awareness and knitted his fingers together in a pose of feigned relaxation. "Yes, of course. Tell me, Commander," he said, resuming his normal acerbic tone, "is this preposterous experiment absolutely necessary?"

"Not at all. We could reach Betalon under conventional power. But even at top speed the trip would still take us over a year. Of course, if you don't mind spending that much time with us—"

"You've made your point, Smith," Rondell said petulantly. "Get on with it."

Jason glanced over at his first officer and saw Clark give a wink of approval. They were all as anxious to be rid of Rondell as he was to be through with them. To Brant he said, "Commence recharge of power circuits one and two for final leap." Turning to the communications console he said, "Better check our passengers. I don't want any space-sick travelers when we make our next jump."

Lieutenant T. R. Cosgrove was the communications officer of the *Eclipse,* and had transferred along with Jason Smith when the mission began, as had First Officer Clark. But their last ship had been the *Adrian Dar,* a sleek fighting cruiser of the Twelfth Stellar Fleet, and not a space-leaping cargo cruiser. With his thick crew cut of light-brown hair and his childlike features, the lieutenant looked more like a raw recruit than a veteran of more than a score of battle engagements in space. As he made a methodical check via voice circuits of the thirty men in the passenger compartment his expression remained studious and somewhat indrawn.

Finally Cosgrove spoke briefly into his headset mike and turned toward Jason Smith. "Only two are feeling sick, sir. I told them to adjust their equilibrium stabilizers."

Jason nodded. "Good."

At that moment, another person aboard the *Eclipse* took advantage of the brief delay. A voice called out through Oleg Rondell's personal communicator.

"What's going on up there?"

The voice belonged to Zelig Farand, a leading figure in world commerce and the business adviser on the mission. He also was in the labyrinth of niches that took up half of the passenger compartment below.

"Nothing unusual, just a routine test of the system," Rondell said, suddenly playing the experienced space traveler. "In another fifteen minutes we should be there."

"Glad to hear it," Farand's voice said. "Presuming of course that Smith gets us there in one piece."

Rondell was certain both his own voice and that of Farand were reaching Jason Smith's ears. "Oh, I imagine he can handle a *cargo* ship safely."

"It's a wonder he wasn't dismissed from the service after that disaster on Pelos Nine. And now a diplomatic trade mission"—Farand laughed coarsely—"what poetic justice."

The words had reached Jason's ears, all right; there were few on the operations deck that had not heard the exchange between Rondell and Farand. But he gave no indication of it, other than leaning back once more into the gel-lined chair.

The memories of Pelos Nine were still there, all too clear in his mind. He had been leader of a squadron of fighting cruisers in the recent war between the Earth's forces and those of the Alturian system. Tall and trim, he had been the youngest squadron commander in Earth's space history, but it was a natural achievement for the highest-scoring cadet the academy had ever trained. And promotions had come fast during the war.

Pelos Nine—when the long war ended . . . and almost flared anew.

Unavoidable as it was, the treaty violation still demanded a scapegoat. Unjust or not, the blame had fallen on Jason Smith. Stripped of his squadron, held in limbo for a month while the bureaucrats tried to decide what to do with him and his crew, Jason would likely have lost even his rank and commission had he not volunteered for the experimental test flight of the *Eclipse* which preceded this mission. And now here he was on his way to Betalon, newly contacted planet on the fringe of the galaxy.

This was his first diplomatic and trade mission, and one he did not greatly like. He was playing ferryman and nursemaid to Rondell and Farand, and thirty honor guard soldiers whose sole purpose in the mission was to serve as window dressing for the ceremonies. Tin soldiers for diplomatic games. The thought irritated him like a raw sore.

His thoughts were interrupted.

"Power circuits one and two fully recharged, sir," Brant called out from the engineering console. "We're ready to go."

"Fine," Jason said. "The sooner this is over, the better."

First Officer Clark fed the new coordinates into the navigational computer. Despite the immensely greater distance to Betalon, the leap would take no more time than the test run. If time could even be considered a factor . . .

"Open power circuits one through twelve."

Brant tapped the controls. "Done, sir."

New field patterns were formed deep within the cruiser. Its mighty engines were poised and ready. The ship itself seemed to anticipate the mighty surge of power that would snap it to its destination, and the flooring shuddered faintly.

"Activate," Jason ordered.

The great throbbing of the engines began again, this time with far greater power than before. It built to a high-pitched whine that engulfed the cruiser, making further conversation impossible. In his niche, Oleg Rondell braced himself and cursed silently. He could not be heard anyway.

The whining sound reached its peak. The outlines of the cruiser became indistinct as before.

And then the jolt!

For a moment the men's minds hung in an abyss of infinite emptiness, devoid of all thought, all feeling. Then suddenly an unexpected flash of light.

The space leap had been made, but something was wrong. Something was drastically wrong.

Jason jerked forward in his chair and stared at the view screen. He could hardly believe what he saw. The contours of a strange planet occupied three fourths of the screen, and were rapidly covering the remainder. The *Eclipse* was in a high energy dive and aiming straight for the planet's surface.

Clark's expression was more astonishment than alarm. "There's been a bloody malfunction!"

"*Brant!*" Jason shouted. "Recharge the circuits immediately."

"Impossible, Commander—we'll crash before we have enough energy stored for even a minimal leap! That last jump took all of our reserve."

"That's not the worst of it," Clark added, studying his indicators. "With our engines' negative field, we're being sucked into that planet's gravity field at incredible speed."

Jason studied the figures flashing on the forward wall. Their altitude reading was a blur, impossible to read.

"Then void the power circuits! Get rid of that negative field. Use pulse energy to slow us down. Use all of it, in one burst."

Brant looked grim. "But we'll have none left for a landing!"

"Do it anyway. About all we have to choose between right now is a soft crash and a hard one."

The *Eclipse* went screaming down into the planet's atmosphere at a velocity that would have incinerated the ship if not for the protective shields. Inside, the crew was safe from the fiery descent, but it would be a brief safety if they impacted at that speed.

Brant activated the pulse energy circuits and readied them for firing. The power would be channeled in a single burst, fired in the direction of their movement. Reluctantly, he tapped the control that would release their total store of landing energy.

Instantly, a shrill blast rocked the cruiser. The *Eclipse* was deflected from its sharply angled descent into a glancing trajectory. The incredible velocity diminished, and would diminish more as the cruiser began to push through the deeper layers of atmosphere. But there could be no normal landing with the pulse energy depleted.

Details of the landscape now became clear on the domed view screen. The crew stared silently at the hypnotic image before them. Gigantic mountain ranges rolled by beneath them, to be replaced by great stretches of dense jungle. Green growth seemed to be everywhere, except in a few strangely blighted areas where nothing grew at all. Areas that bore the colors of festering death.

The surface was looming closer. Impact would come within a matter of moments.

Jason switched on the ship's master intercom. "Attention all hands," he said. "Prepare for emergency landing. Repeat—*prepare for emergency landing*—"

CHAPTER 2

SIGNAL FROM NOWHERE

The massive cruiser hurtled on, skimming another mountain range below. Great jutting rocks reached up to claim the *Eclipse,* but the gleaming ship missed them by scant meters.

Past the range of towering rock in mere seconds, the cruiser now raced onward into the lower level of a shallow valley. Here, in the flat land past the base of the mountain range, a dense forest of green leafy plants grew to a height that dwarfed the cruiser. First the tops, then lower branches were wrenched off as the *Eclipse* tore through the foliage. The supple vegetation did little harm to the hull of the ship. If anything, it helped to absorb some of the momentum, acting as a drag on the craft.

With a shrill scraping sound that tore at the nerves, the ship plowed through perhaps a kilometer of dense surface vegetation, creating a deep rille of soil in its wake. At last it came to rest, thudding against the base of one of the enormous plants. Deep within the heart of the *Eclipse* a weird groan ebbed outward and the ship, which had until now stayed rigidly upright, lurched ten degrees to one side.

With the last falling branch came an awful woe-filled silence. Dust and debris slowly settled in the air, catching bits of sunshine. Light came filtering down through leafy openings and made bright patches on the ship.

And all was deathly still.

But there was still life in the great ship. Secondary power circuits had recharged sufficiently to maintain light and life-support systems. For many long minutes there was no movement within the operations compartment. Then—

Jason Smith struggled to move. He was still deeply embedded in the gel-lined chair. His hand sought the release switch, found it, and the protective lining oozed back away from him. With effort, he leaned forward. He regretted the move instantly. His head reeled and he had to steady himself for a moment before he could rise from the chair. The dull, aching throb in his head told him to stay still for a moment, but he wanted to check his crew and passengers.

A low moan came from behind him, and Jason turned in time to see Rondell tumble from his niche and collapse in a heap on the flooring. The hefty diplomat gained his feet, weaving groggily, and leaned against a bulkhead for support.

"Commander—"

The voice brought Jason's attention quickly around to the first officer's console, where Clark was struggling to get free.

"I can't release from the chair," he said. "The bloody switch won't activate."

Jason moved forward, carefully at first while he adjusted to the slant of the flooring. He reached Clark's side and tried the release switch himself. It still failed to operate, so he located the backup switch in the side of the chair and pressed that. After an instant's delay, the lining oozed back.

"Are you all right, Danny?"

Clark took a moment to assess his state of health. "I believe I'm quite unharmed, sir. I confess, though, my head's a bit muzzy."

"So's mine." Jason gave him a pat on the shoulder and helped him up.

Lieutenant Cosgrove was stirring in the next seat over. He released from his chair and got to his feet. He almost fell.

"Hey!" he said. "What happened to the gyro?"

"Crash must have knocked it out," Jason said. "Could have been worse."

He glanced around the operations deck and saw that the other crew members were getting to their feet, apparently unharmed. But there were others below.

"Lieutenant Cosgrove, if your commo circuits are still working, check with the passenger section—see if there are any injuries."

"Right, Commander."

Jason turned. "Brant—can you get any damage readings on the engines?"

The flight engineer checked the circuits on his console, with no response. The display screen was blank.

"Negative, sir. Everything's out."

"You'd better get down there and check. If it's something we can fix, we may be only a day late."

As Brant departed, Jason said to Clark, "Check the computer records—see if you can find out what went wrong."

"Right, Commander."

Jason's attention fell on the view screen in the forward wall. It was still glowing with color and light, but since impact the image had been completely scrambled, and there were intermittent flashes that accompanied a faint arcing sound from somewhere within the system. Jason switched to a backup circuit and the image cleared.

On the dome was displayed a 180-degree view of the forest. Even reduced on the view screen, the effect was overwhelming. The immense treelike plants extended as far as the eye could see, their smooth green trunks reaching up to a canopy of foliage a hundred meters above them. And what lay beyond the forest?

"What if it isn't something simple, Commander?"

Jason turned to face Oleg Rondell. The diplomat was still leaning against the bulkhead to steady himself, and for the moment at least there was none of the usual sarcasm in his voice.

"What?"

"The engines," Rondell explained. "What if the problem is something you can't fix? If the damage is irreparable, then what?"

Jason did not reply. He stared at the view screen image and pondered the alternatives. There were not many.

"Commander," Lieutenant Cosgrove said at that moment, "we've got nine injuries in the passenger section. Some of the safety devices must have failed."

"Anything serious?"

"Just one—a soldier named Benson. They don't know if he has internal injuries or not, but the med tech is checking him. The rest of the injuries are mostly broken arms and legs."

One fifth of the men disabled, Jason thought. At least the operations crew could still function. Assuming they still had a ship to function *with*. He stepped over to where Clark stood at the computer console. Looking over his first officer's shoulder, he could see that there was still barely enough power to operate the circuits there.

"Find anything yet?"

Clark looked up. "Hard to say, sir. There's no indication in the sensor records of a malfunction in the engines or guidance systems. Assuming, of course, the sensors were doing *their* job." He pointed at one of the small display screens where a graph was depicted with a high peak in an otherwise straight line. "But there *is* that."

Jason frowned. "What is it?"

"That's the scale which monitors energy levels outside the ship. It shows perfectly normal levels, except for here"—he tapped the surface of the screen for emphasis—"where it shows a power surge, right about the halfway point of our leap. The computer offers no specific data or conclusions, but it must have been an extraordinarily high energy field to register that much."

"Big enough to deflect us off course?"

Clark shrugged helplessly. "As I said, sir, it's hard to say. With a system this experimental, there's still a lot we don't know."

Jason considered it. "Then it could have been a star going nova near our trajectory, or almost anything."

"Not quite *anything.*" Clark's look was puzzled. "A nova or most other natural phenomena would look more random or show a wider tapering off of energy. But look at that peak, sir—as neat and precise as if a draftsman had drawn it there. I really can't explain it."

"I suppose we may never know. But I'll tell you this: we're going to check the system over from top to bottom before we even *think* about making another leap."

"Quite understandable."

"Commander, if I may interrupt . . ." Oleg Rondell walked toward them, holding onto the equipment consoles and whatever else was nearby to steady himself. "We *must* contact Earth and inform them of our crash."

"All in good time, Representative," Jason told him. "All in good—"

"Sir," Lieutenant Cosgrove interrupted softly, "there's going to be a problem with that."

"What now?"

Cosgrove swallowed hard. His commander looked as if he had quite enough burdens, thank you, without having a new one pointed out.

"Well, it's just this, sir," he began. "Our long-range communications equipment is the only means we have of contacting Earth. And that requires a lot of power, from our primary circuits. So until we get those fixed, we're not only stranded, we also can't call home."

Rondell fumed, straightening the decorative shoulder caps of his formal jacket. "This is insufferable! There *must* be a way to get help."

Jason ignored him for the moment. "Lieutenant, you still have enough power for communications on the planet's surface, don't you?"

"Yes, sir. But who are we going to call? I saw no signs of civilization on the way down."

"Our descent covered only a small area. If you had landed in the old jungle regions of Asia or Africa, would you have any idea that cities such as London, New York or Tokyo existed?"

"I suppose not. I'll get on it right away, and scan for any local signals, too."

The remaining technicians in the operations compartment had been methodically checking their instruments and controls, and Jason now quickly conferred with them one by one. There were backup circuits for many of the ship's functions, but each check revealed the same thing: massive power failure of all circuits essential to space flight.

Oleg Rondell had ceased relying on surrounding objects for support. His self-assured posture had returned and he began to walk nervously about the operations compartment. Finally, his patience seemed to evaporate and he approached Jason Smith.

"This is a complete waste of time," he said. "You should be conserving what power we have instead of wasting it on a futile search for assistance here. Even assuming there *are* aliens on this world, they may not be advanced enough to help us."

"I suspect they are," Jason said. "On the way down I saw a few areas of land that looked as if they had been used for testing radiation weapons of some kind."

"Weapons?" Rondell tasted the word and decided he did not like it. "That's not good—not good at all. If they're hostile they might easily overwhelm us."

"This may be a diplomatic mission, but we're not without weapons of our own."

"Of course, but why invite trouble? No—in my opinion we should avoid any transmissions until we can contact Earth."

"Thank you for your opinion," Jason said. "It has been duly noted. Now if you'll excuse me, I have other matters to attend to."

With that, Jason headed for the navigation console, leaving Rondell to fume. At that moment, Zelig Farand emerged from the elevator which had brought him up from the passenger compartment, and entered the operations deck. He was limping slightly and his bald head bore a small medical dressing, but beyond that he seemed to have no serious injuries. Farand glanced about the area with a bewildered look, then his gaze fastened on the forward view screen and he stared hard and long at the alien landscape revealed there.

Rondell joined him, sizing up the man's minor injuries. "I see you are one of the lucky ones."

"Lucky?" said Farand. "I suppose. After that crash we are lucky just to be alive. What happened?"

"I don't know," Rondell said. "I don't think Smith does, either. But something threw us off course, right into the gravity field of this planet."

"Probably a miscalculation." Farand glanced toward Jason Smith. "Mission Command should never have chosen him for this assignment."

Keeping his voice low, Rondell steered Farand away from the others. "I doubt it was a miscalculation. Smith and his crew have an exemplary record except for Pelos Nine, and that unfortunate incident was not caused by incompetence, just bad timing."

Farand looked taken aback. "But you've always said—"

"Never mind that! What I say publicly or for Smith's ears is strictly in keeping with official policy on the matter. Besides, whatever self-doubts Smith may still have about the incident are exploitable. He's a strong-willed man, and I intend to keep him under my thumb."

"Even so, under the circumstances, I would feel better if the command of this mission was turned over to someone else. In fact, we should demand it."

"Think it through, man," Rondell chastised him. "Aside from the two of us, everyone else on this vessel is a military man. If we press the issue, the crew members will certainly align themselves with Smith. Besides, if Smith remains in charge then whatever goes wrong will be on his head instead of ours. Then when we return to Earth and make our report, Smith will be taken care of once and for all."

Farand considered it, a thin smile forming on his lips. "Perhaps I've underestimated you, Oleg. All right, then. We'll play this your way . . ."

At the navigation console, oblivious to the conversation which concerned him, Jason Smith conferred with First Officer Clark. "Cerus Major?" he said. "That's it, then?"

"It would seem so, Commander," Clark told him. "The star charts match up. It's an essentially Earthlike planet, the largest of two in the Dromii system."

"Ever been explored?"

"Negative, sir. Not even by automated probe."

"Too bad. It would be nice to know what to expect." Jason tapped a set of coordinates into the computer. He frowned at the answer which sprang forth in glowing numerals. "We're about as far off course from Betalon as we possibly could be."

"I would say so, sir," Clark agreed. "But of course, the extra distance won't matter much, once the engines are working."

"The distance doesn't matter at all, now."

The voice came from behind them, and they turned to see Brant approaching. The *Eclipse*'s flight engineer dusted his hands before folding his arms in a posture of grim resignation.

"What is it?" said Jason.

Rondell and Farand approached. They seemed to sense bad news in Brant's manner.

"It's the number two engine," Brant explained. "It tore loose from its mountings during the crash and smashed into the primary chambers."

Jason closed his eyes and shook his head slowly. Clark said, "That finishes it."

"What's the matter?" Rondell asked. "Can't the engine be placed back in position? Can't it be repaired?"

"Representative," Brant explained, "we've got thirty tons of transspace engine down there, jammed into the primary chambers where the power for space flight, for long-distance communications, for almost everything important, is stored. Even if we could somehow move it, which we can't, we still couldn't repair the damage with the tools and equipment on board."

Rondell's facade of confidence fell away totally. "Then we are stranded. And there's no way we can even contact Earth or a rescue ship."

"Stranded," said Farand. "But won't they even look for us?"

"Where would they begin?" Jason told them. "Search the entire galaxy? I doubt it."

A silence fell over them. A silence broken a moment later as Lieutenant Cosgrove suddenly straightened at his console.

"Commander," Cosgrove said, "I think I've got something."

Jason turned to the young communications officer. "Not more bad news, I hope."

"No, sir," said Cosgrove with an odd look as he faced them. "It's a radio signal, from somewhere on the planet. It matches none of the standard codes. It's like nothing I've ever heard before. . . ."

CHAPTER 3

INTO THE UNKNOWN

The sounds of the alien jungle were suddenly augmented by a new sound—a high-pitched, piping note, cool and electronic, wavering rhythmically with certainty and precision. It repeated continuously, seeming to convey no message and to have no discernible purpose. Yet its very existence offered hope.

Lieutenant Cosgrove adjusted the controls on the small, portable tracking scanner he held, from which the sound emanated, and studied its tiny display screen. He stood with most of the *Eclipse*'s crew on the broad surface of the massive boarding hatch. The ten-by-seventeen-meter platform revealed an opening of equal size in the hull of the great cruiser, which had been made level by the extension of its telescoping stabilizer legs.

"The signal's definitely coming from the northeast, Commander," Cosgrove said. "About forty kilometers from here. Maybe fifty; hard to tell without triangulating it."

Jason Smith glanced at the display screen on Cosgrove's scanner, then turned his gaze toward the northeast. Dense jungle growth lay ahead, and in every other direction for that matter.

"It'll be rough going," he said. "A good three days' journey."

"At the very least," First Officer Clark agreed. "It's a pity we don't have a skimmer aboard, or even a land vehicle."

"They weren't deemed necessary. Not for Betalon."

"Maybe not," Clark said, his eyes darting in Rondell's direction. "But whatever bureaucrat made that decision, he's a bungle-minded idiot for not anticipating an emergency!"

Rondell knew he was not the one responsible, but his face colored anyway. He had been paying close attention to the conversation without appearing to, and he chose now to voice an opinion.

"Commander, listen to reason! There's nothing to be gained by this expedition."

Jason was removing his decorative commander's coat. The steamy semitropical region was too hot for the nonessential elements of the Starforce uniform. He said, "I'm well aware you don't approve, Representative."

"Approve? Of course I don't approve," Rondell snapped. "It's too dangerous, I tell you. What if you don't come back?"

"I'm touched by your concern."

Rondell bridled. "You know very well what I mean, Smith. Your responsibility is here with us."

"My responsibility is to get us all safely back to Earth—nothing more, nothing less. And I can't do that just sitting here waiting for a rescue ship that will probably never come." He paused to accept the webbing harness and equipment Clark handed him. "It's time you faced facts, Representative. Our survival here is now our main concern. That radio signal seems to indicate the presence of a technologically advanced culture. If friendly, they may be able to assist us. If they're hostile, we have to prepare for the possibility of attack. Either way, we must find out."

"And what if this 'technologically advanced culture,' as you call it, decides to attack us while you're gone?"

"You've got weapons, and we're only taking five of the honor guard soldiers with us. As long as you maintain standard security procedure you should be all right."

Rondell simmered inwardly now. "I only wish I shared your optimism."

Clark handed the stout diplomat a computer-printed checklist, and said, "You should have enough food and supplies for several weeks. If we're not back with help by then, you'll have to find which of the local plants are edible. Brant's had training in that area."

Rondell looked the list over without comment. He was glad enough at the moment to be considered in charge of the remainder of the crew, even if it was temporary. Had he known that Brant had orders to take command should there be trouble, he would have felt considerably less pleased.

Jason slipped the webbing harness over his shoulders and secured the fasteners. With the deft ease of a Starforce soldier going into action, he adhered a force gun, an interrupter and other items of equipment to the webbing. He then checked the seven men who were about to embark with him on the exploratory expedition, to be sure each had his gear and his rations. All seemed ready.

"We'd better get started," Jason told them.

"Right, Commander." Clark quickly moved to a control console on the boarding hatch and twisted a dial halfway around. With a sudden humming of servos, a panel opened in the edge of the thick hatch and a telescoping ladder extended, section by section, to the ground below.

The eight men descended, one after the other, until all were standing on the firm soil of Cerus Major. They paused while, above, Brant activated the controls to raise the ladder. There was no point in leaving an open invitation for unwelcome guests.

Brant called down, "Good luck, Commander."

Jason threw him a glance that took in the still glowering Oleg Rondell. "To you, also. We'll call you at dusk. Otherwise, maintain radio silence."

"Understood, sir."

With that he turned and started off into the jungle, the others following. When they had covered roughly a hundred meters' distance, Jason stopped to look back at the great cruiser he had commanded for so short a time. It was the one tangible element of Earth's civilization and security, and they were leaving it behind. Would they ever return? That question was obviously in each man's mind, but no one gave voice to it.

In silence then, they resumed their march, plotting a course as straight toward the source of the mysterious signal as the terrain and the vegetation would permit. Jason led the way, with Clark and Cosgrove immediately behind him.

They marched in a standard defensive pattern, every other man with his weapon facing to the left or to the right, ready for the possibility of attack. All carried hand weapons, and the soldier in the middle of the loose formation shouldered a force cannon.

The device, a long tube with power and energizer circuit frame surrounding its center, had ten times the power of the small force guns. Its pellet pod held only fifteen of the large energy globes to the hand weapon's thirty small ones, but each of the large globes held enough stored energy to rip apart even the thickest polyceramic armor plate.

The landscape that surrounded them was remarkable in the extreme. Incredible in their variety, the plant forms that thrived in this part of the planet taxed the mind. A multitude of subtle shapes and colors had developed over the eons. Some of the plants were remarkably like those of Earth and the other planets which bore Earthlike atmospheres and soil, but others were like nothing else anywhere.

Great bulbous growths of fungus material, red-topped and supported on sturdy stalks of whitish brown, towered over the men from Earth. Blue-and-lavender creepers were draped from virtually every treelike plant and worked their way through the maze of vegetation, adhering to every plant they touched with sticky tendrils.

A myriad of flowers, some large enough to engulf a man, filled the air with an overpowering scent that mingled with the pungent smell of moist soil and grasses. And as the men worked their way onward, it took an unexpected amount of willpower to press on to their unknown destination, rather than merely standing and gazing in awe at the beauty around them.

"Incredible," Clark said as they marched, his head swiveling to take in the view. "Just incredible! The place is a veritable Garden of Eden."

Jason nodded, but kept a wary eye on the terrain. "Maybe. But just remember, even Eden had a serpent."

"True enough, Commander. True enough."

They now reached an area where their path was blocked by a dense growth of vegetation. Jason snapped his interrupter from its place on his webbing harness and thumbed it on. From the small, palm-sized device a needle-thin beam leaped out. There was the usual hissing sound as the beam ionized the air through which it passed, then a crackling rustle as it sliced through the foliage more swiftly than a sharp knife. Severed branches and leaves fell like rain, and in a moment the path was clear.

Jason paused a moment to wipe his brow. The heat was not really oppressive, but it was enough to dampen their uniforms with sweat. He was about to continue when something made him glance upward.

Below the highest canopy of plant growth, the great treelike structures, was another level of vegetation. Slender rods reached up to a height of twelve meters, surmounted by large spheres of coarse growth in which blossoming flowers protruded. Against the light of the sky, the bases of these spheres were only silhouettes, but he thought he had detected movement in the instant he looked up. Now, he saw nothing.

His eyes might be playing tricks on him, he thought, and his nerves as well. He started forward again.

"Lieutenant Cosgrove, are we still holding true to course?"

The young officer cradled his force gun in the crook of his arm while he used both hands to operate the portable tracking scanner. "Yes, sir. The source of the signal is still dead ahead."

Also ahead, at a short distance, lay another obstacle. Stretched across the only clear path before them was a twisted tangle of vines, curiously swollen in great bulges along their lengths.

"My turn, Commander," Clark said, and moved ahead of the others. Holding his interrupter at arm's length, he quickly aimed and fired a beam at the center of the strands. The vines instantly parted and collapsed to the ground in heaps. Clark started to pass on through.

That was when all hell broke loose.

A weird sound filled the air, a sound that was like a thousand whispering voices, or a muffled continuous chirping. Simultaneously, something came flying out of holes in the large swollen bulges of the vines. The things—living creatures or whatever—had the appearance of pale-blue puffballs the size of a man's fist. The fast vibratory movement of the hairy fibers made them a blur in the filtered light of the jungle.

The puffballs were circling outward in an increasingly larger arc, probing sightlessly, apparently searching for the defilers of their homes. In seconds there were at least a hundred in the air, with more still emerging.

"Danny—look out!" Jason shouted.

The warning came too late. Clark was already in their midst, and even as he tried to get clear two of the puffballs collided with him, one against his hand, the other against his leg just above the boot. Instantly, the things convulsed against him and Clark let out a yell before slapping them off and crushing them into the ground.

The remaining puffballs continued to fan out, their circling paths taking them nearer to the other men. What had been curiosity quickly became alarm as Clark's reaction to the attack alerted them to danger. To a man, the soldiers broke formation and dove for cover, snapping out their interrupters and opening fire.

Hissing and crackling, the narrow beams slashed back and forth through the air above them, occasionally crisscrossing as the puffballs came within range of more than one man. The strange flying creatures withered away into nothingness as the beams struck them, and in less than a minute nearly half of them had been destroyed. The rest scattered, perhaps sensing defeat and seeking new vines to bloat and inhabit.

In the next moment, Janson was on his feet and running to aid his first officer. Clark was on his knees as Jason reached him, looking pale and wincing with intense pain.

"Commander," he gasped, "the bloody beggars can *sting*."

"Take it easy. Let's have a look at it."

Clark extended the stricken hand, and Jason looked at it with growing horror. A deathly green pallor was spreading upward from the wound, following the veins of the wrist.

"My leg"—Clark indicated the spot—"one of them got me there, too."

Jason pulled Clark's personal antitoxin device from its place on his equipment harness. Each device was adjusted to its owner's individual body chemistry.

Still holding the device, Jason pushed Clark's sleeve back away from his wrist. The green pallor had progressed farther than he thought. It had already passed the elbow and was still advancing. If it reached his heart—

Jason placed the device against Clark's shoulder, well above the spreading pallor. Pressing the switch, he fired a dose of antitoxin directly through the sleeve and into Clark's shoulder in an almost microscopically thin stream. He immediately reapplied the device to Clark's leg and repeated the procedure.

All he could do now was wait. The antitoxin device had been designed to work against virtually every type of nerve agent, animal venom and plant poison in the galaxy, but there was always the chance that it would prove ineffective against some new alien form. As an added precaution, he injected extra doses of the antitoxin near the site of each wound.

"How's he doing, Commander?"

Jason looked around and saw that Lieutenant Cosgrove was standing behind him, a look of concern etched on his boyish features. The three of them, with their shared experiences aboard the *Adrian Dar,* felt a stronger link than any of the newly acquainted honor guard soldiers could feel.

Jason turned his attention back to Clark. "We should know soon."

In five minutes' time the progress of the green pallor had stopped and it began to fade. Normal, healthy color began to appear once more, and as Clark massaged the muscles of his arm and leg, the look of pain on his face eased dramatically. Jason felt confident that the danger was over, but still he wished to give his first officer adequate time to recover.

As he helped Clark to his feet, he asked, "How are you feeling?"

"Better now, Commander. Much better." Clark dusted himself off and got his gear back in order. "Shall we press on again?"

Jason looked ahead, his eyes searching the path before them. "Not just yet. There's a clearing just ahead, and I think we're about due for a rest break."

Clark seemed about to protest, for he sensed Jason's concern and was not one to hold up the progress of the others on his own account. But as he studied the fatigue showing in the expressions and postures of the inexperienced honor guard soldiers, he realized he would be doing them more of a disservice by arguing to continue.

Finally, he said, "As you wish, Commander."

Judging from the position of the planet's sun overhead, it was midafternoon. The eight earthmen sat on the ground in the midst of the clearing and relaxed as best they could, cooling off in the mild breeze and resting their feet, as all foot soldiers have been wont to do since the first armies marched. All of them consumed a portion of their rations and water brought from the *Eclipse,* and Clark was no exception.

While the ship's first officer chewed quietly on the dry ration wafers, he busied himself with another task. Instead of drinking his water directly from his canteen, he instead poured some of it into a metalloy cup taken from his supply kit, then adhered a small heatpak envelope to the cup's bottom. Pulling the activating tab on the envelope caused the chemicals inside to combine and react, and in a matter of moments the cup became so hot that Clark had to set it down on a flat-surfaced rock near him.

Jason and some of the others were beginning to watch now, their curiosity getting the better of them. Seemingly oblivious to this attention, Clark waited a moment as the water in the cup began to steam, then carefully dropped in two small tablets also taken from his supply kit.

Cosgrove raised a bushy eyebrow at this. Leaning closer to Jason, his voice was a whisper. "Commander, isn't that water we brought from the ship?"

Jason's voice was equally low. "I'm sure it is."

"Then he doesn't need to boil it," a perplexed Cosgrove said. "And he *sure* doesn't need to add purification tablets to it."

"I wouldn't think so."

Clark, meanwhile, produced a metalloy utensil from his kit and proceeded to stir the concoction, whereupon the water began to darken to a deep brownish amber. Not at all the sort of reaction one might expect from water-purification tablets.

Wrapping a large leaf about the cup for insulation, Clark now raised it to his lips, sniffed the fumes questioningly, then took a speculative sip. By now, he had fully aroused the curiosity of all.

Clark swallowed. "Well," he said, seeming to sigh inwardly, "it's not a proper cup of tea, but I suppose it will have to do."

Jason broke out in a grin. "Tea? I might have guessed."

Lieutenant Cosgrove attempted to swallow his laughter, finally turning away self-consciously to recheck the signal on his tracking scanner. His chuckles soon infected the others.

Clark looked up, with surprise and mild consternation. "Well— what's up now? Did someone tell a joke?"

There was no immediate answer, for everyone was too amused to reply. Clark, more than a little perturbed, took another long sip of his beverage.

"Space-happy," he muttered to himself. "They've all gone blooming space-happy."

He had started to down another swallow when a great crashing sound from the vegetation beyond gave him a start. He set down his cup, his hand going automatically to his hand weapon. "What in blazes was that?"

The sound came again, and all laughter stopped. The men froze, silent and alert.

Jason listened intently. He could hear movement through the dense plant growth. The sounds came from in front of them and from both sides. Only in the direction from which they had come was there no sound of approach.

Plant growth was being crushed heavily underfoot. Whatever nature of beast it was that stalked them, it was large and there was more than one. How many, Jason could not be sure.

"Form a defensive ring," he shouted. *"Fast!"*

Instantly, the men leaped from their frozen positions and formed a circle, their backs to the center. Seven of them formed the ring of defense, crouched and ready, weapons drawn. The eighth, the man with the force cannon, stood in the center, ready to fire over the circle in any direction it might be necessary.

Suddenly, a hideous, guttural scream tore through the jungle. A second joined it, even closer to the men, and it was quickly followed by yet a third.

The wall of vegetation at the edge of the small clearing abruptly parted ahead of them, to the right and to the left. Torn apart with a suddenness and violence that was nerve-shattering. And through the gaps of shredded plant growth came three lumbering beasts, moving inexorably toward them. . . .

CHAPTER 4

A NIGHT OF HORRORS

The strange alien creatures that approached them had the size and bulk of Earth bears, but they could not be called bears by the wildest stretch of the imagination. They walked upright on their rear legs, which were powerful-looking and as thick as a man's torso. Their bodies were covered with thick, matted fibers, dark green in color. Red stripes ran down from the neck along the arms and upper torso, and the immense handlike appendages at the ends of the arms were shaped like the claws of a crab, and lined with countless sharp barbs. It was not hard to imagine them tearing apart their victims with a single lunge.

But of all the hideous features the beasts possessed, the most terrifying was the head. Here, the matted fibers bristled in a pulsating movement. The huge mouth, a straight slash like a shark's, bore row upon row of teeth, constantly exposed to view. And poised above that open maw was its eye, or what must have served as one. A flattened hemisphere of milky-white substance looked down on them, unblinking, expressionless, terrifying.

"Energize field circuits," Jason snapped. "Link-up!"

Responding to the command, the men each activated a disk-shaped apparatus on the front of their webbing harness. As the units began functioning, an energy field arose around the ring of men. Each man's unit became a part of the whole, and the invisible wall of power took form. The force field was proof against many weapons, and carried a high charge to thwart physical contact, but it would allow to pass anything coming from within the circle.

"Shall we open fire, sir?" one of the soldiers asked.

"Not yet," Jason said. "They may *look* like unholy terrors, but we can't initiate an unprovoked attack."

Someone grumbled something about regulations. Insubordination or not, Jason felt inclined to agree with them.

"It's a pity," Clark observed dryly, "that we don't have Representative Rondell with us. Perhaps he could negotiate with them."

Jason did not smile. "From the look of them, I suspect they would find his flesh more palatable than his diplomacy."

At that moment, the approaching beasts halted. Not more than seven meters away from the men, they would encounter the force field in another three meters. They stood there, staring with their single eyes and studying the men. For a full minute they waited.

Jason then noticed an increased movement in the bristling fibers that covered the heads of the creatures. Almost at once, a strange and powerful scent swept in upon the men. Something in the air irritated their skin and eyes, and affected their muscular control. The men fought to keep their balance.

"They manufacture some kind of gas," Jason said abruptly. "They're trying to disable us. Prepare for attack."

The words were hardly out of his mouth when the creature directly in front of them suddenly lunged forward. With two quick steps, it covered half the distance and would have been upon them in an instant had it not encountered the wall of energy. When its outstretched arms entered the field there was a crackling sound and the creature jerked backward. A small haze of smoke rose from places where the force field had singed the matted fibers.

Instantly, the second creature lunged toward them, getting one third of the way into the field before it too fell back. Again the beast's coat of fibers was singed, but otherwise it seemed unharmed.

Now the creatures grew bolder, slamming into the field two at a time, entering it halfway and then three quarters of the way before falling back. Once more and they would be inside.

Jason could no longer doubt the intention of these strange beasts. Another second's delay and he and his men could be torn apart. He armed his force gun for midrange power and ordered the others to follow suit.

"Ready," he said. "One burst only. *Fire.*"

A pellet whizzed out from his force gun with deceptively slow speed. It caught the foremost creature square in the torso as it started its next lunge. At the instant of contact, the pellet released its one hundred Roorson units of kinetic energy with tremendous impact. The beast was hurled violently backward for a distance of five meters.

The other men had achieved similar results with the two beasts that charged on their sides of the circle. But the results were temporary. Almost without hesitation, the monstrous things regained their balance and charged again.

A second burst of pellets toppled the two that approached from the sides. But the one that came from the front had bristled out its coat of thick fibers and the pellets that struck it released their energy upon striking the fibers, failing to transmit their full impact to the creature.

It lunged forward, slamming through the force field. A wild thrust of one of its claws knocked Jason's force gun from his hand and threw him and the next man off balance. The huge barbed append-ages probed through the air, ready to seize and tear.

Clark and Lieutenant Cosgrove whirled from their own positions, arming their force guns for maximum power and firing. As those deadly claws reached down for Jason and the other fallen man, a stream of high-energy pellets struck the creature from both sides.

Instantly the beast was flung into the air like a rag doll. With a high arcing trajectory, it landed seven meters away with a bone-crunching thud. At that moment, it let out a shriek that was alto-gether different, yet even more horrible than its previous growls.

The other two creatures instantly stopped their advance. Turning in the direction of the mortally wounded beast, each trained its sin-gle eye upon it. The creature was lying still and quiet, and the other beasts studied it for what seemed to be an unusually long period. Then they abruptly turned away from the men and approached the still body. Seizing it savagely with their claws, they dragged it into the vegetation and disappeared from sight.

Jason got to his feet and helped the other man up.

Clark asked, "Are you all right, Commander?"

"Yes. That's one I owe you and the lieutenant."

"Always glad to be of service, sir."

The sound of the creatures' departure could still be heard through the foliage. Jason snapped a fresh pellet pod on his force gun and put the partially loaded one back into his pod carrier.

"Come on," he said. "Let's get out of here before they come back for us."

"Just stack them up right there, soldier. And be neat about it."

The young crewman labored under his burden of food-storage crates as he made his way across the *Eclipse*'s cargo deck. He cast a disapproving eye at Oleg Rondell, who had ensconced himself in the elevated seat and control console that would have belonged to the ship's cargo officer during a normal mission.

Rondell sprawled at his ease there, peering down at everyone as if from a throne, and supervising as the lower-ranking crewmen carried out his latest order. A considerable pile had already risen in the center of the spacious cargo deck as food crates, drinking-water pods and other supplies were brought from their usual storage points and assembled there.

The young crewman set down his burden and lined it up carefully with the other crates, though he could not for the life of him see why everything had to be so neat. Pausing a moment to wipe the sweat from his brow, he decided to risk asking a question of Rondell.

"Are—are you sure this is wise, sir? Moving all this food down here, I mean?"

"Wise?" Rondell bristled. "And why wouldn't it be?"

The crewman hesitated. "Well, it's just that it seems unnecessary. And except for the dry rations, we'll only have to turn around and move it all back to the mess compartment whenever we need to prepare something. I don't think—"

"Don't concern yourself with thinking, soldier," Rondell interrupted him. "It's not your function. I want all of our supplies gathered in one spot, where I can keep an eye on them. I don't want everything scattered all over the ship. These matters are my responsibility now, and I intend to see they're done right."

The crewman thought a few dark oaths, but said only, "Yes, Representative."

Shaking his head gloomily, he crossed the cargo deck and started back for another load. As he entered one of the *Eclipse*'s connecting corridors, he saw Brant approaching and gave the ship's flight engineer a plaintive look.

Brant shot him an understanding smile. "How are things going with His Eminence?"

"About the same," said the crewman. He lowered his voice. "Sir, do we really have to take orders from that—that—*diplomat?*"

"Only until the commander gets back," Brant said. "And only so long as his orders don't endanger the ship or the crew."

"It still goes down pretty hard, sir."

"I know, I know. I feel the same way. But let's humor him for now, and try not to give him too much to complain about. Lord knows he'll find enough as it is. And I want you and the others to remember: if a serious problem arises, or we come under attack, the commander has given me orders to take over immediately."

"Right, sir." The crewman smiled wanly. "It's enough to make a man wish for trouble. Well, I'd better go get another load. At least it's better than just sitting around wondering how the others are making out."

"Good man." Brant gave him a comradely slap on the shoulder and went on his way.

The crewman moved on down the corridor and turned the corner, disappearing from sight. As his footfalls faded into silence, a furtive figure moved in the shadows of a cross corridor and cautiously emerged into the light.

Zelig Farand spoke into his communicator. "Oleg, I think there's some information you'll want to know."

Jason again felt the sense of being watched, again from above. He glanced up at the tops of the midlevel stalks, and this time he could clearly distinguish the forms of living creatures clinging to the plants. Tiny things, they were still little more than silhouettes. Yet now Jason could see them well enough to determine that they had four limbs and a long prehensile tail. They resembled Earth monkeys in their appearance and their movements, yet they made not the slightest sound. They only watched the expedition's passage with mute curiosity.

"What is it, Commander?" Clark said.

Jason let his gaze linger upon the creatures for a moment longer, then said, "Nothing, I guess."

Clark glanced up at the creatures himself. "Whatever the little beggars are, at least they seem harmless."

"Probably." Jason arched an eyebrow. "But I've had the impression they've been keeping tabs on us for the past three or four hours."

"Surely not the same ones. The whole area must be full of them."

"I suppose. But I've only seen a few, and never any ahead of us."

Clark considered it a moment, then shrugged. "Perhaps it's just idle curiosity, then. I daresay, to them we must be frightfully strange beasts. *Hello*—what's this?"

A new obstacle stood in the expedition's path. The men had been noticing a gradual change in some of the types of vegetation around them, and now as they pushed through an area of thick foliage they ran smack up against a specimen not previously encountered. What appeared to be a ground creeper of fairly normal form and color ran directly across their path. What made it an obstacle was its size.

Even though perhaps a third of the vine was deeply embedded in the ground, the remaining exposed portion rose to a height of two meters. It was a mammoth cylinder of living plant growth, with root structures reaching from its surface into the soil and twining around nearby plants.

Clark studied the colossal vine with considerable interest. "What do you make of that, Commander?"

Jason scaled the thing easily, then used his new vantage point to look along the vine's length. It stretched out of sight in both directions, weaving through the pattern of foliage and following the terrain. In the distance he could see other vines of the same variety, winding their way across the landscape and disappearing into the distant vegetation.

"It's big, all right," Jason replied. "But no stranger than the rest of what we've seen so far."

Clark joined him on top. One by one, the others followed suit.

Lieutenant Cosgrove checked his tracking scanner routinely, then cast a wary eye above. "Sky's getting darker, Commander. Night must be coming on."

Jason nodded in agreement. "We better find a spot to make camp. We can't risk travel by night."

The men jumped down to the other side of the enormous vine. All were ready to move on, save for Clark, who was still intrigued by the vine's size.

Curious, he pulled his interrupter from its place on his harness. Adjusting it for a short-range beam, he aimed it at the vine.

Lieutenant Cosgrove looked suddenly nervous. "Ah . . . with all due respect, sir . . . I mean, the last time you sliced through a vine—"

"Good thought." Clark stepped back a bit. "I'll be more careful this time."

He shot a narrow beam out, cutting a small circle through the plant tissue. The circular plug fell through, into the interior of the vine, and landed with a muffled *thump*. Unlike the last time, nothing else happened.

Clark approached the opening cautiously. The edge of the opening showed that the plant wall was only fourteen or fifteen centimeters thick. He peered inside, leaning into the opening.

"This thing's hollow—like bamboo," he said, then laughed at the muffled echo that bounced back to him.

Pale-green light filtered through the walls of the vinelike tube. Thin, wispy tendrils hung down inside at scattered points, moving gently in a manner that Clark at first mistook for animate life. Then he became aware of a soft ebb and flow of air within the tube. And a scent. He was sure of it now, a faint scent of spores, of fungus growth, coming from somewhere within the tube.

"Come on," Jason called out. "We can explore later."

"Right you are, Commander," Clark agreed, and started to follow. For an instant he thought he heard another echo of his voice, faint and somehow different.

As he drew away, he noticed that the edges of the opening were secreting sap or some similar substance which was solidifying. It was not merely sealing over the cut surface, but seemed to be growing out from it, replacing the missing plug with new plant tissue in a kind of healing process. In another hour or so, he estimated, the hole might well be completely closed up.

As he set out once again, Clark noticed a large drop of water darken his sleeve with its wetness. Another struck his shoulder, followed by still more. He looked darkly at the sky, from which rain was now beginning to pour, and sighed stoically.

"Just what we needed," he said, to no one in particular.

Darkness fell more swiftly than they had expected. The rain lasted less than an hour, and in an area clear of dense vegetation the men had made camp. Drawing rainwater from a pool that had collected in the collapsed hollow of a large, bulbous plant, they purified it and refilled their canteens.

The iridescent globe of Cerus Minor hung in the night sky, partially obscured by clouds and the irregular patches of higher plant growth. The air was still very humid and mildly warm, and patches of steamy haze rose from the soil and surface vegetation to hang in ghostly clouds several meters above the ground. Too tired for conversation, Lieutenant Cosgrove and the five honor guard soldiers ate their evening's rations in silence.

Forty meters ahead on a high point of land stood Jason Smith, with First Officer Clark at his side. Both men peered through binocular night scopes, seeking openings in the jungle.

Jason lowered his scopes. "Whatever that signal is, it must be coming from that mountain range up ahead."

"So it seems, sir," Clark said, still searching the horizon. "We should reach the mountains in a few days."

"We may not be in shape for a climb by then."

"True enough." Clark lowered his scopes and turned to Jason with a serious look. "What has me worried, though, is the signal itself—the way it just keeps on going, without any change or apparent purpose."

"Maybe it is changing," Jason said, "and our equipment just isn't sophisticated enough to make sense out of it."

"I've considered that. I've also considered the possibility that the signal is nothing more than the emergency beacon of some hapless spacecraft that crashed here the same as we did."

"The thought," Jason said soberly, "had occurred to me."

"Of course, even if that is the case," Clark speculated, "then we may still find something of use in the wreckage."

"Perhaps. At any rate, we have to find out. There's just not much else we *can* try under the cir—"

He stopped short. A scream cut through the night, a hollow, terrible scream. It was all the more frightening because it was not the sound of an alien animal.

It was human.

"That came from the camp," Jason said. "Come on!"

They started back, running at a dangerously fast speed, through darkness that prevented their seeing the uneven terrain they covered. Stumbling more than once over vines and creepers, they kept going. Rigid plants and jutting rocks slashed at them as they passed, bruising their arms and legs.

They reached the camp. All was submerged in inky blackness. Nothing could be seen. The hushed sound of frightened breathing could be faintly heard, and another sound, a weird clicking.

The two men halted. Jason drew a light tube from his equipment pack and activated it. He aimed it at the ground before them and played the beam across its surface.

"Good Lord," Clark exclaimed.

Almost at their feet lay a ghastly thing. Grotesquely contorted, the shriveled form of one of the soldiers looked blankly up at nothingness. There was no doubt he was dead. Only a single wound was visible, near the center of his chest, but his body seemed to have been completely drained of all its fluids. What remained was merely a withered husk.

Weapons drawn, the two men played their lights around the camp area. The beams fell first upon two of the soldiers, crouching in the foliage with their weapons ready, then moved to the other side of the camp to reveal another soldier taking cover behind a large rock. A fourth man was to his right, about two meters away. There was one man missing.

"Lieutenant?" Jason called out.

"Here, sir!"

Cosgrove's voice came from the opposite end of camp. Jason immediately flashed his light in that direction, as did Clark. The two beams fell upon the thing almost at the same instant. A huge black form, coat dully glistening like velvet, stood on six segmented legs.

Two and a half meters tall and at least three meters in length, the insect had Cosgrove pinned to the ground with its forelegs.

The nightmarish creature's intent could not be mistaken. A pointed, tubular appendage where its mouth should be was positioning itself directly above Cosgrove's chest.

Instantly, Jason fired a burst of pellets from his force gun. Clark joined it with a burst from his own weapon.

Several of the pellets missed, but those that made contact sent the giant insect reeling to one side. Cosgrove gained his feet as quickly as he could and scrambled away.

The insect kept its balance and moved awkwardly toward the men, making a peculiar clicking sound with its wings. The two nearest men fell back out of its way. Jason kept his beam trained upon the creature and it seemed irritated by the bright light, its huge eyes better suited to nocturnal hunting.

The insect lunged at one soldier as he ran past seeking better cover, then became aware of the light once more, and moved directly for the source of the irritation: the light, and the morsel which held it.

Jason dove to the ground, rolling clear. Bringing up his force gun, he aimed at one of the rear legs and fired a burst. The pellets hit with full impact and crippled the leg. The thing tilted at an angle, hissing and fluttering its wings madly.

"The force cannon!" Jason shouted. "Use it!"

The soldier beside the rock raised the long tube to his shoulder and energized the circuits. He aimed for the underside of the insect's thorax and fired.

Striking dead center on target, the energy globe erupted in a violent burst of energy, shattering the hard chitin exoskeleton with a terrible sound and slamming the insect backward. It collapsed in a heap, broken and oozing gore. The beast lay still and quiet.

The men slowly gathered in the center of the camp. They stood in silence for a long moment, glad they were alive, yet feeling the loss of their comrade. A shift in wind brought the sound of some distant beast's mournful cry. A reminder that they were far from alone in the alien jungle.

"Everyone, get your gear," Jason said. "We're moving on."

"At night, sir?" one of the soldiers questioned.

"Yes, we have no choice. That insect will attract carrion eaters and who knows what else. We'll have to find a new camp."

The men nodded in agreement, tired but fully understanding the necessity of the order. They quickly moved to get their equipment.

Clark soon returned to Jason's side. Both men stood looking down at the dead soldier's body.

"What shall we do about him?" Clark asked.

Jason considered for a moment. "There's another of those large, hollow vines ahead. We can open a section of it and lower him inside. It will be better than leaving him out here for the insects and scavengers. We can mark the spot."

"Right, sir."

"Let's get started, then."

With lessened spirit, the men pressed on. They had covered another kilometer of terrain when their lights revealed a large outcropping of rock rising sharply from the jungle floor. Jason played his light across the shadowy surface of the stone and the beam revealed a shallow cave. It was three meters across and seven deep, and offered at least some shelter from the elements.

Clark inspected it carefully. "Doesn't appear to have been occupied recently."

"Then we'll make camp here," said Jason.

Jason took first watch, positioned at the mouth of the cave, with the force cannon and extra pellet pods within reach. He wondered how long the nights lasted on Cerus Major. He had determined that from midday to sunset a bit over five and a half hours had elapsed, so depending on the seasonal tilt of the planet, night could be ten, eleven or twelve hours long. And the dangers of the jungle were infinitely greater in darkness.

More time elapsed. It had been five hours by Earth standards since the star that warmed this planet had dipped below the horizon.

A sound came from behind him. He turned and saw one of the soldiers.

"You'd better get some rest, Commander," the man said. "If tomorrow is anything like today . . ."

"All right. If you get tired, wake someone. Dawn may be a long way off yet."

"Right, sir."

The new sentry stared out into the darkness. Now and then, there were sounds of creatures moving through the vegetation beyond, but they seemed to be keeping their distance. Even so, he was glad to have the cave at his back and weapons so near at hand. An hour passed.

New sounds now came, closer than the others, and the sentry

placed his hand on the nearest force gun as a rustling in the foliage attracted his attention. He smiled when he saw what emerged.

"Only a monkey," he said to himself.

The small anthropoid was half a meter in height, with a long tail crooked like a question mark. It was silvery gray in color, and a fringe of whitish fur ringing its face gave it the appearance of a wise old man.

It made no sound, but as it stopped three meters before the mouth of the cave it looked with curiosity at the sentry. The tiny beast began to put on a show, first walking back and forth on its hands, then tumbling over and over like an acrobat.

Amused at its antics, the guard tossed a fragment of a ration wafer to it. Leaping upon the scrap, the monkey examined it closely, then hungrily devoured it. The sentry held another in his hand, motioning.

Slowly, the monkey came toward the offered food. Once in range, he reached out eagerly and took the morsel. As he sat there eating, the guard scratched its head, pleased to have the company of a friendly creature after a day's experience in what seemed a totally hostile world.

"You're a regular pet, aren't you," he whispered to the monkey. "You look pretty smart to me. I think I'll call you Aristotle."

He knew the creature could not understand him, but that did not matter. Having something to talk to would help keep him awake. He felt more encouraged now. When dawn came, he would be ready to start out again, following the others in their search for the signal. And perhaps when they found it, it might even aid in their rescue. He thought of home, and all the things that meant.

Meanwhile, the monkey waited patiently for another scrap of food. When it did not come, the creature began to leap and play, then it scampered up the sentry's back and sat upon his shoulder, letting its tail flick back and forth. Then suddenly it stopped its playing and gazed out into the night at a spot in the dense foliage, staring intently as if listening.

Abruptly, from a hidden place in the folds of its fur, the monkey drew a tiny dagger. . . .

CHAPTER 5

DAWN OF THE EPOS

It all seemed incredibly real. . . .

Jason could sense the padded contours of the command chair beneath him, feel the thrust of the engines propelling them on, see the computer's tactical data flashing by on his display unit. First Officer Clark and Lieutenant Cosgrove were nearby, as were the rest of his old crew.

Moving like a silver dart through space, the *Adrian Dar* closed on the planetoid known as Pelos Nine. Flanked by its fighting squadron, the heavily armed cruiser made its approach from the planetoid's dark side. Below them on the barren and rocky sphere was the Alturian force's key outpost, already responsible for the destruction of many squadrons of Earth's forces.

Jason looked to the forward screen. The image there shifted and took on strange new life as the light amplifiers, infrared scanners and weapons sensors created a composite diagram of the enemy base and its prime targets. With every structure of the Alturian base outlined in vivid, glowing color, there would be no difficulty in aligning their weapons during the assault run. The only difficulty would be in surviving it.

"All ships are combat-ready, sir," Lieutenant Cosgrove relayed from his position at the communications console. "They're all in assault formation."

At his own console, Clark studied his instruments. "I'm getting readings already, Commander," he said. "The blighters are scanning our ships—checking out our weaponry."

"Let them," Jason replied, his tone hard. "It won't matter much, one way or another."

In the next moment, the barrage began around them as the Alturians sought to prevent the ships from penetrating any closer. Billowing flashes of white, searing energy erupted on all sides of the squadron as the ships drew nearer to their objective. The ships' defensive energy shields began to glow and overheat as they neared peak load.

"If we get through this," Clark commented, "their fighters will be waiting for us."

Jason leaned over the controls. "Do we have range yet?"

"In a few seconds more, sir. Just—"

Clark's voice faded abruptly as a blinding flash temporarily wiped the image from the forward screen. Seconds later, charred debris could be seen arcing past the ship's nose.

"They got the *Sun Storm*," Clark said softly. "Cramer's ship. Shields must have collapsed."

Jason's features tightened. "Arm the neutronics."

"Done, sir. I'm turning it over to computer targeting."

Jason keyed in the ship-to-ship voice link. "Begin firing."

At once, each of the remaining ships in the squadron activated their weapons, and a wall of energy erupted into blazing life, partially illuminating the dark side of the planetoid. But even as the deadly beams flashed down at their targets, there came a startled outcry from within the *Adrian Dar*.

"Commander!" Lieutenant Cosgrove shouted with urgency. "A message relayed from Command Base: the Alturians have offered a treaty to end the fighting, and Earth has accepted. We've been ordered to abort the attack!"

On the planetoid below, flashes of light were popping like silent bubbles across the surface. In a moment, there were only darkened splotches of rock where the enemy base once stood. Already, the Alturian fighter craft were dispersing, heading off for other bases, fleeing wedges of copper at the heads of green thruster jets.

Jason leaned slowly back into his command chair, the fatigue of months of battle suddenly settling upon him. "Tell them . . . message received," he said, ". . . too late."

Too late—the words echoed in his mind, and the images whirled and faded into darkness. . . .

Jason awoke with a start, and was momentarily surprised to find himself in the shallow cave on Cerus Major. He shifted uncomfortably against the hard rock, and found his muscles stiff and sore.

Early-morning light illuminated the cave where the rest of the men still slept. The cool, clear light helped disperse the fog of sleep, and was reassuring after the nightmarish quality of the previous day. But the nightmare was not over.

Something was wrong. He should have been awakened at first light. With a quick, instinctive reaction, Jason reached for his weapons. He found none. Every piece of equipment on his webbing harness had been deftly removed.

A swift glance at the other men confirmed his worst suspicions. Each man's equipment had been taken while he slept.

Jason moved to Clark and shook the sleeping officer. "Danny—wake up." Next were Cosgrove and the others. "Lieutenant—everyone—wake up!" Within seconds, they were all stirring, some more alert than others.

Clark seemed to sense the urgency in Jason's tone first. "What is it?"

"All our gear's been stolen."

"*Stolen—*" Clark looked stunned as he reached automatically for the weapons that were no longer there. His eyes flashed to the mouth of the cave. "The sentry—"

Jason was already moving, and was the first to reach the spot. The soldier was still sitting where he had been, though he leaned now against a rock. His head lolled upon his shoulder.

Clark looked questioningly at the still form. "Dead?" he ventured.

Jason said nothing. He checked the man's pulse and breathing, then looked at the pupils of his eyes. At the base of the man's neck he found a small scratch, little more than a nick in the skin.

"He's been drugged," Jason replied at last.

"Drugged?" Clark said disbelievingly. "But by whom?"

Cosgrove came up behind them. "Or by *what,* sir."

Both men looked around, only to see Cosgrove staring out at something past the mouth of the cave. Whirling in that direction, they looked out at the foliage beyond.

From the shadows of the weird vegetation advanced a semicircular line of twenty horses with riders. The mounts looked like a sturdy Arabian breed, trim and finely formed. Their skulls seemed larger, and their manes stood tall and erect like those of zebras, but in all other ways they might have been earthly horses.

More remarkable were the riders. Remarkable not for their appearance, but for the seeming illogic of their position. For seated on the horses were tiny monkeys, none more than a half meter in height, tails curved upward like question marks, and faces fringed with beardlike fur. Strangely, several of the mounts had more than one rider.

They sat not on saddles, but rather clung to the coarsely woven covering that extended the length of each horse's back, beginning in a yoke about the neck and reaching back to the flanks. Most of the coverings were plain, but a few among them were decorated. Affixed to the coverings at spots were holders for weapons, some of them empty now, since the monkeys held pistols of odd design trained at the cave opening. In mesh bags slung across the backs of two mounts were the earthmen's stolen weapons and gear.

The advancing line of horses and riders reached a point where its ends met the stone outcropping, effectively cutting off all avenues of escape. They halted, waiting.

Cosgrove asked, "What do we do now, Commander?"

"Wait here," Jason said. "I'm going to try something."

Slowly, taking care to make no sudden moves or threatening gestures, he walked from the mouth of the cave and approached the line of aliens. He had moved forward about four meters when one of the monkeys in front of him suddenly straightened and leveled his pistol. With a sizzling flash of light and a crackle of sound, a spot of vegetation next to Jason's foot suddenly turned to flame and vaporized. The warning shot passed close enough to sear a small patch of his boot.

Jason promptly halted, then stepped back a pace. "All right, you've made your point. Now what do you want of us?"

There was no answer. Jason had not really expected them to understand his language, but he did wonder why they made no attempt at verbal communication. After a moment, ten of the monkeys scrambled down from their mounts, bringing strong cords woven from vine strands.

Clark came up alongside Jason. He studied the small creatures with a puzzled look. "Now what?"

"I think," Jason told him, "that they want us to surrender."

"Surrender?" Clark was incredulous. "To *those* little fellows?"

"Those little fellows have highly respectable heat ray weapons, and we're unarmed." Jason looked at him pointedly. "What would *you* suggest?"

Clark shrugged, clearly without an answer. He had to admit it would make no sense to try to fight their way clear. They would be gunned down instantly, without a hope of escape.

"Still," he said, "I don't fancy being marched off to some alien executioner."

"If they wanted to kill us," Jason said, "they could have done that while we slept. Who knows, perhaps they're just the local police."

"Somehow I don't find that very reassuring."

"No, but let's play along for now. I don't want anyone hurt, and we might get a better chance to make our move later."

In short order the men's hands were tied securely, all the while under the watchful eyes—and guns—of the patrol. The men were herded into a tight group and made ready to go.

Clark looked down sourly at the ropes which chafed at his wrists and his pride. "Now I know how Gulliver felt."

The patrol party moved out, their captives in the center of the column. Six of the mounts led the column and six followed at the flank, while the remainder proceeded on either side. The soldier who had been drugged had revived but was still groggy, and Jason gave him support as best he could with his bound hands. Clark assisted from the other side.

The column of aliens and earthmen marched on, through the seemingly endless, steamy jungle of Cerus Major. Hour after hour, without a rest, they continued as the mounting heat of the day began to sap their energy.

Jason had been paying careful attention to their course, and several times he had sighted the mountain range that they had pinpointed as the most likely point of origin for the mysterious signal. It did not take him long to reach the conclusion that the patrol was not going toward the source of the signal, but rather away from it, at a tangent to the course of their original expedition. That, added to the fact that none of the aliens possessed any equipment that looked even remotely like communications gear, made it clearly possible that they were not responsible for the signal. And if they were not, who or what was?

"It just makes no sense," Clark said as they marched. He kept his voice low. "These creatures can't be what they seem."

"They do seem unlikely soldiers," Jason agreed.

"It's not only that," Clark said. "Besides their small size and limited brain capacity, they also have some odd contradictions in their technology. Why would a race of beings advanced enough to invent something like those heat ray pistols have to rely on horses for transportation instead of some form of land or air vehicles?"

"It's a puzzle. Of course, it could be said that horses have an advantage over most vehicles in terrain like this."

"Perhaps," Clark said. "And then again, it may be that they've merely obtained the weapons from some more advanced culture here, or scavenged them from a crashed spaceship."

"The source of the signal?"

"It's a strong possibility." Clark shook his head, newly perplexed. "I don't know. And then there's this strange business of their not talking. When they captured us back there, they all seemed to know what to do, yet not a word was spoken."

"Maybe they're all telepaths," Jason said.

Clark frowned mightily. "They're something, all right."

Still they marched. The sun of Cerus Major was directly overhead now. Its rays burned down relentlessly, cooled only by the leafy shelter of the great plants. Abruptly, even this gave way as the column came out upon an enormous clearing that stretched for miles.

Jason and the others stared ahead in wonder. Before them in the distance stood a city. An ancient-looking city whose foreboding walls told of centuries of decay. . . .

CHAPTER 6

THE CITY OF FEAR

Towering structures of time-tempered stone rose above the plain, faintly shimmering in the heat waves sent up by the baked, hard-packed soil. The buildings were simple in design, but were monumental in both their size and in the subtle beauty of their form. But their beauty belonged to the remote past. That much was a certainty, for the magnificent structures of the ancient city had clearly gone uncared for during countless years—perhaps eons.

High walls around the city blocked any view of the ground-level interior. Along the parapets, alien guards on horseback patrolled, watchful eyes turned outward toward the plain that surrounded the city. There was no rock, no scrap of vegetation or surface irregularity, that might offer cover to an approaching enemy or an escaping captive.

"I wouldn't care to try breaking in," Clark whispered to Jason as they marched. "Even with weapons."

"Breaking out won't be much easier. Maybe at night, if it's cloudy. We'll have to see what their security looks like."

The column came to an abrupt halt. They were now only some sixty meters from the outer wall of the city. Jason and the others watched as the apparent leader of the patrol moved forward. Oddly enough, it was one of the creatures on a mount which bore extra riders.

Several of the guards on the parapet had halted and now faced the column. They and the leader of the patrol stood staring at each other, but exchanged not a single word.

The drugged earthman had recovered fully during the last part of the march and no longer needed support from either Jason or First Officer Clark. Clark stood next to his commander and watched the silent confrontation of the aliens with keen interest.

"You may have been right, sir," he said after a moment. "They do indeed appear to be telepaths."

Jason said, "So it seems."

"I wonder if they can read our thoughts?"

"Hard to say. But even if they can, they may not understand them."

Clark appeared puzzled. "How's that again?"

"Our thoughts aren't free of language, Danny," Jason explained. "Our emotions, perhaps, in their rawest state, and other general feelings. But other than that, we still tend to think in words and phrases. Even our logic patterns may be unfamiliar to them."

"I see," said Clark. "So unless they've had a crash course in the King's English, our thoughts could be all gibberish to them."

"For now, let's hope so."

Then, just as abruptly as it had stopped, the column began to move forward. A great gate in the high wall swung inward, revealing an opening into the city. The alien patrol and its captives moved on, through the gateway and the thick wall of stone. With a great moan, the giant gate swung back into place, sealing them inside the city.

Crude dirt roads led away from the perimeter road which ran just inside the wall. Taking the center road, the patrol marched their prisoners toward the distant massive buildings and the heart of the city. Most of the small buildings at the outskirts of the city were deserted, and many were in ruins.

However startling the city may have been after their trek through the untamed jungle, more startling was the scene that now was before Jason and the others. As the column moved through a great arch of weathered stone, a new section of the roadway became visible. In the drainage ditch to the right, a dozen stooped figures worked with primitive hand tools, repairing a section of the ditch. A guard on horseback watched over their feeble efforts. At the patrol's approach, several of the stooped figures turned and looked.

"Humans," Clark said under his breath. "Commander, they look like Earth people!"

Dressed in tattered gray garments, the group of laborers was made up of both men and women, young and old. Jason felt a sudden wave of disgust and anger at the sight of them, forced to do the aliens' menial work. For they had not the look of prisoners. Clearly, they were slaves.

At that moment, Jason saw something that alarmed him. As they approached, the patrol and its captives had attracted the attention of the alien guarding the human slaves. With its attention thus diverted from the laborers, one of the humans, a boy who looked to be in his teens, chose to seize the opportunity to escape. Edging cautiously away from the others, the lad sought to reach the edge of a crumbled building and the alley beyond.

He was taking quite a chance, and Jason tried to think of some safe diversion he might create to give the boy a chance to escape. They were almost even with the workers now, and so far none of the aliens in the patrol seemed to be paying any attention.

All that changed abruptly. In almost the same instant, several of the aliens at the head of the column looked toward the boy, and the guard and its mount turned back around. At once, the boy broke and ran, scrambling over the rubble at the base of the ancient building. If he could reach the edge of the ruined wall, he might still get out of sight and elude them for a time.

But even as the boy leaped up for the edge, the guard took aim with its weapon and fired.

"*No!*" Jason shouted.

In his fury he started toward them, unthinking of his own danger. He had not gone more than two steps when hands seized him, restraining him.

"You can't help any, sir," Clark told him quietly. "It's too late for that."

The boy hung for an instant at the top of the low wall, his body twisted in pain and the blackened spot on his back where the heat ray struck still smoldering. Then he began to slip down to the ground, fingers clawing helplessly at the hard, unyielding stone.

"Too late," Jason said, his voice hard and bitter. "Always . . ."

The other laborers were near panic. Some seemed ready to run, anxious to reach the boy and find out if he still lived. But the guard instantly moved his mount to block their path, waving his weapon threateningly. With fearful eyes still darting in the direction of the fallen lad, the others finally moved back, cowering before the alien guard. Reluctantly, they returned to their work, picking up their tools in hands already bruised and swollen from labor.

With order restored, the patrol moved on. As they marched, Jason seethed inwardly. Whatever doubts they might have had about the aliens' motive in their capture, those doubts were now gone. He knew he and his men could expect only one thing: enslavement. And if their appearance on Cerus Major presented too great a mystery, then they might also expect to be tortured for information about themselves. And if the aliens learned of the *Eclipse* . . .

Occupied buildings were becoming more numerous. The amount of activity they were encountering indicated that the patrol was nearing the inner section of the city. More and more aliens could be seen, always on horseback, or near their mounts. And the humanlike creatures could be seen as well, laboring at many tasks, and always guarded.

Crossing the road ahead of the patrol, a line of the humans was pulling a large, crudely made wagon, piled high with grain and vegetables. In the distance, other wagons could be seen being pulled from an outlying area that had been cultivated for several different crops.

Buildings rose a hundred meters into the air in this section of the city. Mammoth structures all, they seemed not to be in use above the ground floor. Most disturbing of all about the strange and alien city was that for all its activity, there was an awesome silence. Only the sound of the wagon's creaking wheels as it rolled past interrupted that silence. No voice, no outcry or shout, no laughter. Only the oppressive silence of fear.

The column drew to a halt before a large building near the center of the ancient city. Forcing Jason and his men ahead, the aliens rode directly inside the building. The structure was as impressive inside as out, with five-meter ceilings and doorways four meters high. The men were taken to a room near the outer wall of the building, untied, and under the threat of the deadly heat ray pistols forced to go inside. One of the monkeys touched a control on the wall and hidden mechanisms closed the massive door. Then the patrol departed, the clatter of their mounts' hooves receding down the corridor.

Lieutenant Cosgrove leaned against the wall, and the four remaining honor guard soldiers sat down on the floor, too weary after the long march to stand.

Jason paced around the room, examining every corner. Except for the one locked door through which they had entered, there seemed no other exit. In the outside wall, long, narrow windows cut through the stone, and had been barred with thick metal straps that appeared to be a recent addition. Light and air freely entered the room through the open spaces, but no human could squeeze through.

Clark joined him at the window. Examining the bars there, the young Englishman tested their strength.

"These are pretty tough, Commander," he said. "But we might be able to break a few loose."

"We'd better," Jason said grimly. "I'm afraid we can't count on rescue from the ship. The others won't even know something's happened until we miss our next scheduled radio contact tonight. And even if they sent a search party out, I doubt if they could track us this far."

"Whatever we try, we'll have to wait until dark. There are too many patrols to risk moving about by day." Clark was looking out the window at the passing aliens, and a thought suddenly struck him. "Nothing but soldiers. You know, this isn't a city—it's a ruddy military camp."

"Strange," Jason said after a moment. He was staring out through the window at a different angle from Clark's. "What do you make of that?"

"Make of what, sir?"

Jason pointed to a plaza less than a hundred meters from them. Gathered around what must have been an ancient fountain were perhaps fifty or more of the monkeys, most of them either lying or sitting on the ground. Their movements were slow and feeble, and their appearance suggested old age. They were also the one exception to the rule that the creatures were never without mounts. Occasionally, a monkey would ride by on horseback and toss a handful of vegetables to the begging creatures.

"They don't take very good care of their own sick and elderly, do they," Clark said. "Frankly, I'm not surprised."

"It's not just that," Jason said. "Look at the way they're acting: like monkeys usually behave. Not at all like the others."

Clark contemplated it a moment, then finally turned away from the window with a tired shrug. "They're probably just senile."

Jason finally turned away from the window himself and sat down, resting his feet and legs. As he leaned back against the wall, he realized suddenly just how very tired he was.

Half an hour passed. Jason dozed briefly, then came quickly alert as Cosgrove called out:

"Commander—"

The lieutenant was at the window. Jason moved toward him.

"I thought you'd want to see this, sir," Cosgrove told him. "It looks like the patrol's caught someone else."

Jason peered out, half afraid he would see some of the others from the *Eclipse* being brought in. But this was not the case. The patrol had only one prisoner, and a most unusual one at that.

There in the center of the patrol, arms bound and closely guarded, a young woman marched in silence, a look of solemn defiance on her pretty face. She was as startlingly human as the other beings they had seen earlier, but it was clear that she was not one of the cowering slaves who did the aliens' bidding.

Tall and slender, the beautiful young woman wore strange garments of greenish hue, a color in direct contrast to the red of her full, long hair. And it was not the kind of rust-brown or auburn hair that passes for red on Earth. This was the bright hot red of leaping flames.

Clark had joined them at the window, and most of the other soldiers had taken up a position at the other window. All watched the patrol pass for as long as the angle of the narrow windows would permit. It was apparent that the patrol was coming toward the very same building in which the earthmen were held. As they listened, the sound of hooves in the great hall beyond told them that the prisoner was being brought inside. Minutes later, the heavy door grated shut in the next room, and the sound of the aliens receded.

Jason listened a moment longer, then said to Clark, "There must be several groups of humanoid creatures on this planet. If we're mistaken for one of them, then our captors may not be so curious about our sudden appearance."

Clark nodded. "That might buy some time for the others back at the ship."

At that moment, a sound from the hall alerted them that alien guards were returning. They moved to the far wall, opposite the door, and waited. At the touch of a control outside, the wall mechanism rumbled and the massive door swung slowly open. Several of the guards on horseback were in the hall outside. One of the monkeys scrambled down and entered the room. It leveled a heat ray pistol at Jason's head, then motioned toward the door. Jason stood his ground for a moment, and the monkey motioned again, this time more threateningly.

"I guess I'd better go with them," Jason told Clark. "Keep an eye on things while I'm gone, Danny. And if I don't come back, you're in charge. . . ."

CHAPTER 7

THE BEAST KEEPER

The sun of Cerus Major still bore down with afternoon heat as Jason Smith was led from the ancient building to the street outside. This time they did not tie his hands as before. The aliens seemed confident that there was no risk of escape here in the midst of their city, and in fact, any attempt to break and run from the guards would have been nothing short of foolhardy.

In a smaller formation this time, they marched him down the main thoroughfare and past the fountain where the old and unfit monkeys begged for scraps from passersby. Jason studied the guards as he walked, seeking the answer to the aliens' strange behavior. His gaze was met with the same expressionless stares he had seen before on the guards' faces.

He glanced back at the fountain. As old and feeble as those monkeys were, he thought he saw more life in their eyes. Something, an intangible quality that was somehow different from the guards. He gave up the train of thought and resumed studying the buildings, streets and alleys of the city, creating a mental map for future reference. He hoped he would have an opportunity to use it.

Ahead, a great building stood out among the other structures in the city. An enormous round wall of stone reached up, its surface carved with symbols of alien design. Some of the symbols appeared to represent humanoid creatures, yet there were subtle differences between them and the humans Jason had seen thus far on this world.

Curving around the sides of the structure were stairs and ramps leading up to openings in the wall located more than halfway to the top. Aliens on horseback could be seen entering the building from several sides. Perhaps it was a place of government, or a meeting chamber. Or maybe something else. . . .

Rather than going up one of the ramps, as he expected, the guards led him around the side and to a ground-level entrance. The scale of this building was like that of the other, with high ceilings and wide hallways. The same blue-gray stone had been used to form its walls. Yet there was a difference. Something in the air itself suggested a dread purpose, and the almost tangible presence of death.

An odor, musty and pungent, became more pronounced as they turned from the hall and descended a long ramp, moving into the depths of the building. The cool clammy feel of underground chambers offset the heat from the outside, but the stillness of the air made the atmosphere even worse than the warmth above.

Strange globes filled with a phosphorescent liquid illuminated the hallway. Jason could make out what appeared to be cells along both sides of the hall. Carved slots in the doors admitted little light into the cells, but in some of the narrow openings faces peered out. Human faces, full of despair and fear. The place stank of sweat and excrement, and it was clear that not even a rudimentary form of sanitary equipment had been provided for those being held in this . . . this . . . *dungeon*. Far from being a seat of government, this place had the look of a jail. Or something far worse.

They turned down an intersecting hallway and proceeded to a chamber at its end. Fastened to one of the stone walls were chains and manacles, and with these Jason was shackled in place. The guards checked the bonds, then quickly remounted and rode back down the hall, leaving him there in the semidarkness.

Minutes passed slowly. Jason began to wonder how long they planned to leave him here, and how soon the torture might begin. He tested the strength of the manacles which held him, tugging against the pull of the chains. But except for bruising his wrists, the effort accomplished nothing.

At that moment, a faint sound came to Jason's ears. A soft sound, as of rock scraping the floor. It came from the wall directly in front of him. As his eyes strained to see the source of the sound, he became aware of a panel in what he had thought to be a solid stone wall. The panel swung slowly open into the chamber, and as it did Jason braced himself for whatever might come in.

What came through the opening was a man, or what seemed to be one. More than a head shorter than Jason, the stocky man who entered the chamber wore a loose-fitting robe that was little better than those of the human slaves, but around his neck was a thick and official-looking medallion that clearly set him apart from the others. A fringe of hair ringed his bald head, and his eyes were wide set and beady, staring in the semidarkness at Jason. He reached into his robe and brought forth an object which proved to be a small phosphorescent globe. Holding it in the air to better illuminate the small chamber, he peered intently at the captive.

"Ho! A new face for the trials!" he said. *And he said it in perfect English.*

Jason was astonished, but he was also suspicious of anything that might happen in this city. And he was not sure he could trust even his own senses in this place.

"And what crime have you done, friend?" the stocky man continued. "Rob someone else's ration of food? Try to escape, did you? Tell me, now. Makes no difference to Old Stod. I don't make the laws around here."

Jason watched the man but did not speak.

"Strong silent type, are you? One of the swamp people, maybe? Well, I've seen plenty of those come through here. They're like that, they are." The man looked Jason over more closely now, noticing with special interest his well-made uniform and boots. "No, maybe I guessed too quick. You wouldn't be one of the swampies. No, sir, not with those fittings. You're a strange one, all right, a strange one indeed."

"Who are you?" Jason said abruptly.

"Ha! So you do speak!" the man said. "But obviously you do not listen. I am Stod—Old Stod."

"Perhaps I should have asked instead, *what* are you?"

"Well, I am not a criminal, and I am not bound to the wall with chains, as you are." He smiled faintly. "What I am is the keeper of justice."

"I thought you said you didn't make the laws."

"Oh, I don't. No sir. Such high privileges are not for the likes of us lowly humans." He pointed toward the ceiling. "The big brains up there make the laws."

Jason did not know whether to humor this strange little man or not. There was more riddle than sense to him. "Yet," he said, "you are the keeper of justice?"

"Oh, yes indeed!" He walked to one side of Jason, fixing him with a look of cunning. "But justice comes in many forms, you know. Many forms, indeed. Small, large, powerful, weak. Sometimes it is dark and terrible, creeping up on you, unknown, unseen . . . deadly!" Stod drew closer as he spoke, his voice nearly a whisper now, his fingers moving clawlike and menacing as if to illustrate his point. "Sometimes it is bright and clear, right there before you, but you can't escape it. Sometimes it crawls on many legs, sometimes few. And I can pick which one you'll get. Oh, yes—there are many forms of justice. And I keep them all down here, in chambers big and small, waiting for troublemakers like *you*."

Jason was trying to decide if the little man was insane, or only tauntingly cruel. Whatever the case, he seemed to hold the key to at least some of the mysteries confronting them. Assuming there was sense to any of it. . . .

"You were born in this city?" Jason asked.

"Yes, a good many years ago. Even before the big brains came here and took over." He sighed. "Only those of us my age remember what it was like then, and there are few left now. Why do you ask?"

"Because you speak my language."

"Of course, and you speak mine," Stod replied. "Would you be less surprised if I didn't?"

Jason ignored the question. "Why are you free when the other humans are slaves?"

"None of us are free. Oh, no, friend, not here. Not anymore. It's just that I have certain privileges the others do not."

"Privileges," Jason said, "given in return for what?"

"You ask a *lot* of questions." Stod looked him over again. "Very well. I receive privileges because I am talented. You might say I have an uncommon ability with certain creatures. Creatures the big brains find most useful."

Jason arched an eyebrow. "The justice you spoke of?"

"Exactly." Stod smiled. "You are a clever one, friend. Perhaps if you do well at the trials you may find a place here. Working *with* the big brains is better than working *for* them."

"Cooperating with those slavers isn't exactly what I had in mind."

Stod frowned reproachfully. "Stranger, I don't know who you are or by what misfortune you are here, but let me tell you this: The Epos do not look kindly on unruly humans."

"The Epos?"

"Our lords and masters. The local gods, as it were." He paused, disbelieving. "Oh, you *must* be a stranger here!"

"What do the monkeys have planned for us?"

"The monkeys?" Stod's face held an amused look. "Then you don't know, do you? Well, I won't be the one to tell you. As for what the Epos plan for you, I can only guess. Judging from your strange appearance, I suppose they may take you to the Citadel after the trials. If, that is, you *make* it through the trials."

"How do these trials work?"

"Oh, they're quite simple, really. Criminals are brought here, like you have been, then they're taken upstairs to the arena." He looked thoughtful. "Place used to be a theater of some sort, I think. A long time ago, of course, back when the old ones who built this city still lived here. The big brains use it to help keep the humans in line. I think they even find it amusing." Stod gestured toward the ceiling again. "Anyway, up there you'll meet some of my creatures. If you fail to combat them successfully, well . . ." He shrugged.

"What if I don't fail?"

"Well, of course, if you triumph over them you will be free of whatever charges they have against you, and allowed to join the labor force. Although in your case, they may have something else in mind. You seem to be quite a puzzle, and the Epos, they don't much like puzzles."

At that moment, a sharp buzzing sound disturbed the relative stillness of the chamber, making Stod straighten with a jerk. The sound seemed to come from the medallion around Stod's neck, and Jason realized that the large decorative ornament must have some kind of electronic device within it. And judging from Stod's reaction, the signal had come from his masters.

A voice came from the medallion next, a voice that was flat and metallic. A harsh voice of command.

"We are ready for the next human. Prepare your beasts."

Stod bowed his head respectfully, even though the gesture could not be seen by those who called him. "Yes. I shall obey."

Jason had a hard time equating the powerful voice which came from the medallion device with the tiny creatures which had taken him and his crew captives. It had to be artificially produced, triggered somehow by the thoughts of the telepathic creatures. A bridge to span the mental gap between themselves and their trusted slaves.

Stod turned and went back to the open panel in the wall. He stepped through, then hesitated and looked back at the bound earthman. He smiled faintly, and Jason could not tell whether the expression was genial or merely mocking.

"You're not a bad one, friend," Stod said. "In fact, you're rather interesting. Tell you what: the first creature I'll send out will be a brill. Quite an intelligent beast really, and terribly dangerous. But they do have a weakness of sorts. A word of advice: keep an eye on its breather gills. They always snap closed just before it starts to make its killing move. See you, friend."

With that, the stocky little man disappeared into the dark passage beyond the opening and the panel swung shut. The wall once more appeared to be solid.

With Stod's puzzling words still ringing in his ears, Jason was startled to hear the sound of guards returning to the chamber. They rode up on their mounts and dismounted, unshackling the manacles which bound him to the wall. In the next instant, a grating sound above his head made him look up.

Light flooded the chamber as a section of the ceiling slowly slid to one side, revealing the glaring alien sky. A ladder was thrust down from above, and one of the guards in the chamber motioned to it, encouraging him to ascend with quick, threatening moves of a heat ray pistol.

Jason looked up again at that glaring patch of daylight, and wondered which fate was the worse. . . .

CHAPTER 8

BATTLE WITH A MAN-KILLER

Climbing the ladder through the opening in the chamber ceiling, Jason found himself at ground level in the center of the giant circular structure. As his eyes adjusted to the bright light of the open-air arena, he became aware of a low stone wall circling the field of combat, behind which rose a series of tiers like giant steps. Gathered along the tiers, like spectators at some great sports attraction, were the aliens and their mounts. Looking around, Jason tried to estimate the number of them. There had to be at least a thousand. Were they all judges for the "trials" or merely observers?

Almost as soon as he asked himself the question, Jason noticed a section of the gallery that was different. Decorated in a manner suggesting the mark of alien officialdom, the special tier held what appeared to be the high-ranking members of the culture. A puzzling aspect of the scene was that although the horses were lavishly decorated, the monkeys were sharing their mounts, with three or four of the small creatures to each horse.

He might have pondered longer on the puzzle, but a sudden cessation of activity in the gallery made him sense that the trials were about to begin. He turned slowly, looking for the direction of attack, and waiting for his first glimpse of the thing called a brill.

He did not have long to wait. Ten meters ahead of him, a movement attracted his attention. An opening had appeared in the ground, revealing a pit or chamber like the one in which he had waited. At first, nothing stirred. Then there came a hissing, rasping roar like the rush of air through monstrous jaws, and the beast emerged.

Fully a head taller than Jason, the brill was a remarkable breed of insect life, apparently taken from the jungles beyond the plain. Surprisingly, the creature balanced its bulk on two slender legs. Large multifaceted eyes seemed to see in all directions at once, and the double pincers of its mouth clicked open and shut menacingly. The head and thorax of the brill were fused together, and the bulky body tapered down to a narrow abdomen where the legs joined it. Top-heavy and awkward in appearance, the creature moved with startling grace and agility, its frontal grasping appendages poised and ready to strike.

A grating sound behind Jason told him that the opening to the chamber below him had been sealed. There was to be no escape back the way he had come. He moved slowly, carefully, as the beast stalked him, studying the creature's patterns of movements. He wondered how he could be expected to combat such a terrible opponent without even a weapon to defend himself.

Almost in answer to his thought, a large cudgel of wood was rolled toward him from the wall. Cautiously, he moved to it, picked it up and tested its feel in his hands. It was a good two meters long, strong and heavy—almost too heavy to be wielded effectively. But at least it was a weapon, and as such, better than none.

Edging closer in slow back-and-forth patterns, the brill seemed to be measuring Jason's ability to follow its movements. Sizing him up, studying his reflexes and timing with a predator's instincts.

Jason searched the creature's head and thorax, looking for the breathing gills that Stod had told him to watch. Or had his warning been merely a trick, a diversion to give him less of a chance?

But the gills were there, gently flexing in and out as the beast breathed, one set on each side of its head. Jason watched them carefully as he moved counter to the stalking pattern of the brill. When would it make its move?

Abruptly, the gills snapped shut.

Jason ducked, diving low to the ground as the brill leaped forward toward him. The beast had spanned five meters in an instant and sailed over Jason, barely missing him with its claws and landing four meters on the other side of him. It turned swiftly and studied the man from Earth.

"So," Jason said under his breath, "Stod was right. At least I've got a chance."

He had learned something else as well: once the brill began its leap it could not alter its direction or speed. Once committed, the creature could only continue along the same path until it landed. That might prove useful. Jason looked to the gallery for some sign of approval for his first maneuver, but attempting to read the faces of the aliens was pointless.

The brill now began to stalk again, moving this time in a sidestepping maneuver that took it almost in a complete circle around Jason. It stopped again, and studied his reaction. Then it began a slow dancelike movement back in the opposite direction.

Again its gills snapped closed.

And again, Jason was ready. As the beast lunged for him, he stepped swiftly to one side. Hurtling past him in the air, the brill's claws came close enough to rip the fabric of his uniform. But this time Jason struck back. Starting his swing even as he sidestepped, he brought the heavy cudgel around in a crashing arc and connected with the back of the brill, just below its head.

Off balance, the creature did not land on its feet this time, but instead plummeted into the ground headfirst, tumbling for a distance of several meters.

Jason again looked to the gallery and wondered if he must destroy this beast to win the first trial. And after that, what? Some other creature, perhaps more terrible, and with characteristics that he had not been warned about. Jason considered several courses of action and decided quickly. He could not play the aliens' game by their rules and expect to win in the long run. And anyway, playing by their rules was not his way of doing things. He had his plan now.

The brill had regained its feet. With a great amount of roaring it was stalking him again, but more directly this time, suddenly all business, as if it had decided to give up its cat-and-mouse games. Jason moved slowly toward the wall which stood before the special section of the gallery where the high officials watched. He moved with cautious backward steps, keeping a watchful eye on the brill. For his plan to work, he would have to use split-second timing.

Advancing toward him, the beast followed his movement to the area immediately before the high officials' tier. Its features were more animated now, its jaw pincers clacking together angrily as if enraged by Jason's counterattack. They were both in the position Jason had hoped for.

Watching him, the brill waited for some indication of further movement. It seemed to have taken a defensive posture, waiting for Jason to make the first move. For it seemed to reason within its wary insect brain that if this puny human were tricked into bringing the attack to it, there would be a better chance for a killing strike.

Jason realized he could not risk a further delay. He would have to make the first move and hope that his reflexes were fast enough to be able to execute his plan. He yelled at the brill, jerking his body suddenly, faking the start of a lunge.

Instantly the brill responded. As its gills snapped shut, it tensed and sprang directly at him, hurling its full weight in a violent leap. Its claws reached out, ready to seize and destroy.

It was exactly what Jason wanted. With a swift movement he slammed one end of the cudgel against the ground, ducked low and held the other end aimed at the creature. Bracing himself, he prepared to spring.

The brill collided directly against the raised end of the cudgel, the wooden surface striking the center of its thorax. Jason immediately jerked the pole backward with all his might, letting the beast's own momentum aid him.

Sailing five meters into the air with the combined force of its leap and Jason's cudgel thrust, the brill slammed into the tier of high officials, scattering them. Panicked by the deadly beast in their midst, the aliens fell over each other, some toppling from the tier, and most ending up in confused pileups of horses and monkeys. Armed guards raced their mounts in from the other sections of the gallery to subdue the brill, and throughout the arena the aliens seemed on the verge of a stampede.

But Jason did not stand by and watch the confusion. At the moment the brill had landed in the tier, he raced across the open ground toward the chamber from which the beast had emerged and dove straight into the pit, letting the darkness swallow him up. Rolling with the fall to absorb the impact, he regained his feet and looked around the chamber. As he had thought, it was empty. He knew they could not have stored any other creatures in the same place as the deadly brill.

Finding the chamber door, he located a mechanism that operated it and swung the panel open. Apparently the aliens had not bothered to hide the mechanism since the beasts could not conceivably operate it.

The hallway outside was deserted. Pale light from the phosphorescent globes illuminated the way. Jason advanced down the musty corridor, watchful for any sign of movement.

On either side of him more cells were arranged along the hall. But these were not for people. From these cells came weird and terrible sounds, and animal odors of appalling strangeness. Jason wondered what kinds of creatures the aliens kept there for their perverse amusement. He hurried on along the corridor.

As he walked, sudden movement to his right alerted him to danger. A robed figure was ducking into a side hallway. Jason lunged after the figure and tackled it. His captive put up no fight. Jason pulled him to his feet and held him against the wall. The light of a nearby energy globe shone on the man's face.

Old Stod trembled in Jason's grasp. "Why . . . why, friend—I see my advice helped you defeat the brill," he gasped. "You have won the first trial."

"And the last!" Jason said. "Now how do I get out of here without being seen? *Tell* me, quickly."

"I—I can't!" Stod whined. "If they knew I helped you escape, it would be *me* out there in the arena next."

"It would probably be poetic justice."

Stod's hand reached up surreptitiously, his fingers grasping for the thick medallion hung about his neck. Jason noticed the attempt and quickly snatched the signaling device out of his reach, slipping its chain over the old man's head.

"You're good with words, Stod. You'll talk your way out of any trouble, I'm sure of that!" He tightened his grip on the man. "Now tell me how to get out of here."

Stod shrank back against the wall, seeming to consider. Finally, he said, "All right . . . all right, if you don't hurt me."

"Which way?"

"Follow this hallway to the end. It intersects with another corridor. There is a panel on the far wall, to the left a ways. Open it and go inside. You'll find a tunnel that leads from the arena to one of the buildings across from here. It's unoccupied. You will be able to escape from there."

"If you're lying—"

"I'm not! Just go—quickly. If I'm seen with you, my fate will be sealed."

Jason released his hold on the man and watched as Stod scurried off into the darkness of a corridor. He dropped the medallion to the ground and ran down the hallway Stod had indicated. Another corridor did intersect with it, and Jason went to the far wall. The panel was a short distance to the left. Now, if the beast keeper could be trusted, there would be a tunnel behind it. And if he could not? Perhaps alien guards waited there, or one of Stod's deadly creatures.

He would have to risk it. Jason opened the panel and plunged inside. He closed the door quickly behind him, and waited a moment for his eyes to adjust to the darkness of the tunnel.

Advancing slowly at first, Jason felt along the wall as he went, probing carefully with his feet the ground before him. It would be all too fitting in this place out of the dark ages to have deep pits along the way, or some other fatal trap. But he found nothing in the first ten meters he covered.

To his rear, the sound of alien guards searching through the corridors made him increase his speed almost to a run. Jason covered fifteen more meters of the tunnel, then suddenly ran into a stone wall. The entire surface was smooth. Nowhere could he find a door or panel of any kind.

If not in the end wall, he reasoned, perhaps the door is to one side. He checked the right side first, feeling every inch of the wall's unyielding surface. Finding . . . nothing. Now the left side. At last his fingers located the edge of a panel. Jason pushed it open a fraction. Pale light filtered through.

Jason peered out, then drew a quick breath and held it. In the room beyond, less than a meter away, was one of the alien guards on horseback. The creature was facing in the other direction, or else it could not have helped seeing him.

Jason tensed his muscles. He could not wait for the alien to leave, if indeed it would. Quickly, he swung the panel open and leaped forward. Before the diminutive guard could turn its head, Jason swung his arm hard, striking the creature squarely. It was knocked from the horse and struck the nearby wall. It collapsed unconscious to the floor, dropping its weapon.

Jason ran over and scooped up the small pistol. Now at least he was no longer unarmed. He was planning his next course of action when a sound came from behind him.

What he saw was totally unexpected.

At the moment he had attacked the guard, the creature's horse had skittered to one side, startled by Jason's presence. But now the animal was advancing on him. Its posture was fully alert and tensed now, and its blazing eyes held a look of anger and menace that seemed out of place with its equine features. Teeth bared, the horse suddenly charged. Jason leveled the captured handgun. It felt small and toylike in his hand. He fired.

The horse toppled to one side, breathing heavily. It did not move, yet there was no apparent wound. Jason examined the pistol, and saw that it was different from the heat ray guns he had seen before. Apparently it was a stun or paralysis weapon. The horse would be immobile for a while.

Correction, he thought. Not the horse. *The Epos guard.*

For that was what he had so abruptly realized. The dominant creatures were not the monkeys, as they had assumed, but rather the horses which bore them about. An intelligent equine race that had mastered the tiny creatures which served as their extensions by telepathic command. That would explain why the most decorated "mounts" carried more than one "rider." The highest-ranking guards were simply entitled to more mind slaves.

Jason went to the horse's side and looked over the equipment attached to the woven covering on its back. He recognized a heat ray pistol and removed it. Other pieces of equipment were there also, but their purpose and manner of operation were unknown to him. He decided the two pistols would be enough, and placed them in his belt.

Jason hurried up to the ground level of the building. Risking a look outside, he saw a number of guards in the streets heading for the arena. This was encouraging, for it meant that they still assumed he was hiding out in the maze below. That might give him the time he needed.

The stairs of the building could be ascended by an earthman, even though the risers were on a larger scale than earthly steps. Jason now knew why the aliens did not use the higher levels of the buildings. It was simply too difficult for the horses to go more than one or two flights. Stod's story about the city was apparently true. Another race of beings in the planet's dim past must have built it, to a scale in keeping with their own size.

Jason reached the third floor, then went on to the fourth. On the fifth floor he left the stairs and entered one of the rooms along the outer hall. Windows here faced another building located just across a narrow alley, and leaning out one of them he found an ornamental ledge a meter below him.

A few aliens passed by in the street below, but did not look up. Jason eased out through the window and onto the ledge. Across the way, a similar ledge on the opposite building reached out, shortening the gap. He would only have one try at it, and if he missed, it would be a long fall to the ground below. The gap was not so far that it could not be jumped, but Jason wondered if his muscles would still serve him well enough after all he had gone through so far.

He braced himself against the ledge, aimed and leaped out. Sailing across empty space, his feet missed the ledge and he started to drop. There was a sickening feeling in the pit of his stomach as he felt himself begin to fall. Then as the wall moved up past him he grabbed frantically for the ledge with his hands, and barely managed to catch hold. He held on tightly, breathing hard, his heart pounding.

Slowly, with a good deal of effort, he pulled himself up to the ledge and over the top. He entered the window there, then paused inside for a moment while he regained his strength.

He had to press on. He must get as far away from the arena as possible. Even as he moved through the halls and rooms of this second building, he considered plans. Plans which included returning to the place where his men were still imprisoned and helping them escape. But he realized that his own escape from the arena would make things harder. As long as the Epos knew he was loose in the city, guards would be patrolling every part of the great walled enclosure. Unless, that is, they had elsewhere to look. . . .

Working his way across the fifth floor of the building, he solidified his plan. After crossing what seemed a countless number of rooms and hallways, all of them empty and coated with dust, he reached the other side. This time, instead of merely windows, there was a door as well. It opened onto a covered connecting way leading across the street below to the next building. Jason started across it, grateful for an easier path.

For the next hour and a half, Jason made his way from building to building by means of the aboveground crosswalks that seemed to connect most of the structures, keeping to the upper levels to avoid detection by the aliens. At the outskirts of the city, this procedure had to be abandoned, since the tall buildings appeared less and less frequently. Once more on ground level, it was necessary to move cautiously through the rubble of the ancient structures and, finally, through the drainage ditches that ran beside the roads. Moving, always moving, toward the outer wall of the city.

By the time he reached it, the sun of Cerus Major was at the horizon. Jason had now established that the length of the total day on the planet was twenty-two hours—roughly eleven hours of light and eleven of darkness.

He approached the wall cautiously. Guards circled the parapets at five-minute intervals. He checked his time band to establish the regularity of it, and it held true. There would not be much time to act.

He watched as one of the guards went by and waited until it was out of sight. Moving quickly to the wall, he pulled the heat ray pistol from his belt and took aim at the stone surface. The blistering ray vaporized the rock, and in a little over a minute a hole was cut through the wall, large enough for him to crawl through.

Once outside, Jason stayed close to the wall. He looked across the barren plain at the edge of the forest. The distance was only half a kilometer on this side. He could easily run the stretch of hard-packed soil in five minutes. Jason leaned back against the wall and waited. The next guard would be along within a minute.

Presently, the sound of hooves came softly along the parapet. Jason waited until the guard was almost directly overhead, then leaped out away from the wall and fired upward with the stun pistol. The Epos guard collapsed, nearly toppling from the parapet. Without its master's mental controls, the monkey that had served as its mind slave merely scampered about excitedly and quickly disappeared from sight.

Jason knew his footprints would not show on the hard surface of the plain, and this fact would help in the illusion he wished to create. He looked at the two weapons he had captured. The stun ray was helpful, but the heat weapon would be more useful for a variety of things. Deciding quickly, he took the stun gun, wrapped it in his webbing harness, and hurled the bundle as far out as he could. It landed on the plain, crumpled and dusty, and looking as if it had been dropped by someone in a very great hurry to reach the jungle beyond.

Jason now dove back through the wall opening and headed toward the city. The next guard would be along in five minutes and would report what he found. Jason wanted to be well away from the area by then. Nothing must spoil the illusion that he had escaped.

He crept along the drainage ditches and through the ruins, working his way toward the larger buildings. Once more nearing the center of the city as darkness fell, he entered a vacant building, reached the fourth floor and waited. . . .

In the near-darkness of Primary Scanning Center, an immeasurable distance away, two aliens of larger than human scale studied a round viewing crystal as large as a normal man's outstretched arms. Both were dressed in identical robes that sparkled and glistened with light not wholly reflected from their surroundings, and both were similar in appearance.

The image within the viewing crystal was of Commander Jason Smith, resting now on the fourth floor of the vacant building in the city on the plain. The image was as clear and real as if he were sitting just beyond the round crystal, even though there was no conventional camera device near him to transmit the image. Indeed, everything he had done this day had been displayed here in the crystal. Displayed, and observed.

"Impressive," said the first alien. "Most impressive. I am sure he is what we are seeking."

"Perhaps," said the other. "But there is still much to learn."

"He seems ideal," the first argued, defending his initial enthusiasm. "He has already displayed intelligence, leadership and courage. And even compassion for his enemies: he could have destroyed that last guard, yet he only stunned it. In my opinion, he is worthy."

"Thus far, I would agree with you. But much remains to be seen before we pass judgment. Besides, they still must find our beacon and discover its purpose and operation. Only then may we contact them. You know the rules as well as I, Klon. You helped formulate them."

"Yes . . . yes, of course." The first alien seemed deflated by the other's gentle reminder. He knew his friend was right. Still, an ember of determination glowed softly within him. "But they *shall* succeed, Shom . . . eventually. I am certain of it."

The other turned to him with an understanding smile. "You may well be right, old friend. You may well be right. . . ."

CHAPTER 9

DAUGHTER OF THE RACE OF HOO

An hour after nightfall, First Officer Clark and the other prisoners looked up in stunned surprise at the ceiling of their cell. For there near its center burned a narrow spot of red-hot light, casting its glow over all. Fiery fragments fell from the spot, to land on the floor still glowing with heat.

The cascade of debris abruptly ceased, and the peculiar light of the alien phosphorescent globes streamed through the small opening above the men. Something moved, blocking that light, drawing near to the hole. Something on the second floor of the building which served as a jail.

Softly, a voice called out. *"Danny?"*

Clark hesitated but a moment. "Is that you, Commander?"

"Yes," Jason's voice came back. "Is everyone all right?"

"So far, sir."

"Stand clear; I'm going to cut through."

As the men quickly moved away from the center of the cell, they heard the familiar burning hiss of an alien heat ray pistol. Jason was enlarging the hole with each pass of the beam, and in a few moments had made it large enough to slip through. Careful to avoid the still hot edges of the opening, he dropped lightly to the floor. The men quickly gathered around him.

"Thank God you're alive," Clark said. "How did you escape?"

"I'll tell you later," Jason said. "The important thing is that I did, and I've got three of their heat ray weapons. I took one from a guard I knocked out, and got two more from some kind of a recharging station upstairs. The pistols were plugged into a wall unit, storing up power, and I took the ones that were fully charged. The second floor is in use by the guards as a kind of patrol center, but if we're careful I think we can get past them and out of the building. I created a little diversion earlier, so I don't think they'll be expecting me to break you out.

"And there's something else you'd better know," Jason added. "The aliens who captured us are called the Epos, and we've made a rather large mistake about them. . . ." He quickly explained what he had learned about the telepathic horses and the monkeys which served them.

"An intelligent equine race?" Clark said, mildly incredulous. "Had us fooled good and proper, I admit. That's what we get for not keeping an open mind."

Lieutenant Cosgrove seemed less surprised, his brow knit in thought. "That would explain the cast-off monkeys we saw in the square. The Epos tossed them aside when they were no longer useful."

"They're not long on kindness," Clark agreed. "That's bloody certain. But even with the record set straight on who's in charge, we're still in the same predicament. What do you think our chances are for escape?"

"Reasonably good," Jason said, checking his wrist chronogage, which he had recalibrated for the length of the planet's day. "But if we don't leave this city tonight we may never get out. And there are not many hours of darkness left."

"Well," said Clark, "we're ready to have a go at it, sir."

"That young woman in the cell next to ours," Jason asked. "Have the guards taken her away yet?"

"No, Commander. We would have heard them in the hall if they had."

"Good. I intend to take her with us."

Clark frowned. "Are you sure you want to, sir? I mean, if things go badly, we might just end up getting her killed along with the rest of us."

"I admit there's a risk," Jason told him. "But from what I've seen, her chances aren't much better if she stays behind."

Without another word, Jason went to the wall that separated them from the next cell. Using one of the heat ray pistols, he began slicing an opening in the wall, starting near the floor so that the girl would have time to get clear. When the beam had made a complete circle, he leaned heavily against the block of stone and forced it into the next cell. A quick shove toppled it out of the way. He looked inside.

The girl with flame-red hair was crouching in the shadows of the far corner, motionless and staring. She seemed to be studying Jason and the men behind him with wary curiosity, trying to decide what to do.

With a beckoning gesture, Jason called softly to her. "If you want to escape this place, come on."

Springing from the shadows, she crossed the cell and darted through the opening in the wall. Joining the men, she looked alertly at each one, seeming to search for a face she might recognize.

"Quickly now," Jason said. "We'll have to form a human ladder to reach the hole in the ceiling. Let's move!"

Instantly the men obeyed, gathering in the center of the room. Jason ascended first, heat ray pistol in hand as he entered the second floor room. But it was safe. The room was still empty.

"All clear," he said softly. "Come on."

The girl was sent up next, followed by First Officer Clark and Lieutenant Cosgrove. They helped the next two soldiers up, then the five men together pulled up the remaining two, one hanging by the ankles of the other.

In the increased illumination of the second-floor room, the girl was now able to see the clothing the men wore. Their finely tailored uniforms were a marked contrast to her forest garb of homespun green. Her own trim-fitting robe was of a cloth not unlike silk, her cloak a coarser fabric. Boots fashioned of woven fibers reached up almost to her knees, and like everything else she wore were the color of verdant vegetation.

But these strangers—

Their uniforms were made of synthetic fabrics, and virtually seamless. Their clothes and the technology which made them seemed as far removed from her own people as from the cowering, rag-covered slaves who toiled in this accursed city. Arching a delicate eyebrow, she studied the earthmen with renewed curiosity.

"Of what settlement are you?" she asked, in perfect English, and only Jason was not surprised. "Are you Northlanders?"

"No, we are . . . travelers," Jason told her. "At the moment our home is in the forest. Which is where we're heading if we can escape this city."

"Then please, take me with you. I must return to my people." She stepped closer to him, tall and proud, her gray eyes flashing with intelligence and energy. "I am Laneena, daughter of Shannon the Elder. I am grateful for your help, and if we can reach my village, my people will welcome you and give you shelter."

She was young and vibrant, and her beauty at this close range was nearly overwhelming. There was about her the scent of forest flowers, and her voice was at once both strong and musical. For the first time in his young career, Jason found it hard to concentrate on the job before him. But he quickly forced personal thoughts from his mind.

"I'm Jason Smith," he told her, "and these are my friends. We'll help you any way we can, but I must warn you that what I plan is dangerous. I can't guarantee your safety."

"It doesn't matter. If I stay in this place, the Epos will destroy me to learn what they wish to know."

"All right, then." Jason handed two of the heat ray pistols to First Officer Clark and Lieutenant Cosgrove, keeping one for himself. "Let's go. Keep alert, and move quietly."

He opened the door slowly and checked the hall. No guards were in sight. Silently, the eight of them moved out into the hall. Jason wished there were a closer set of stairs to reach the upper levels, but the only one he knew of was still a considerable distance away.

Fortunately, the patrolling guards seemed to be few and far between, making it possible to cover large distances at a time. Jason led the way, with Clark and Cosgrove guarding the center and rear of the group, respectively.

At last, the entrance to the stairway came into view.

And stationed before that entrance stood an Epos guard! Jason and the others could go no farther around the corner without being seen by the guard. And the longer they waited, the greater the risk of being spotted by another patrolling sentry. Yet shooting the guard also risked discovery.

Minutes passed, long moments that brought the danger of discovery by other sentries closer and closer. They could not afford to wait any longer. Jason raised his pistol reluctantly and took careful aim. He would have to risk it after all.

Suddenly, a hand touched his shoulder. A staying hand that caused him to lower his weapon. Looking around, his eyes met the firm gaze of Laneena. She shook her head in a silent no and pointed at the guard. Puzzled by her gesture, Jason watched as she began to stare in the direction of the alien. Her pretty features tightened in a tense expression as she stared with deep, unfathomable eyes.

Abruptly, the Epos guard stiffened, snapping to attention. No sound was heard, but the creature had apparently received a command. Suddenly leaving the stairway entrance, the guard galloped off along the opposite corridor.

Wasting no time, Jason and the others darted across the hall and into the entrance to the stairs. They swiftly ascended to the third floor, reached the outer wall of the building, and crossed a stone archway. Only when they were in the safety of the next building did Jason turn to Laneena with a question.

"Back there in the hall . . . that guard," he said. "What happened?"

Out of breath, she seemed hesitant to answer, her look still wary. "I told him to report to his superior officer at once. I know some of their words, enough to fool them."

"Told him—how?"

"I can hear their voices inside my head. Only a few of my people can, and I am one of them. We give warning to our village when the Epos come near."

"Then," Jason said, "you're a telepath, too—like the Epos?"

"Telepath?" Laneena considered the word, frowning in puzzled recollection. "Yes, but that is an old word. We call it the gift of silent voices. That is why I must escape the Epos. If they learn I have the gift, they will send me to the Citadel for their scientists to examine. Others of us have been captured and taken there for experiments. None have ever returned."

"This Citadel—where is it? What is it?"

"In the mountains beyond the plain. The high rulers of this city are there, and it is well guarded."

CHAPTER 10

ESCAPE!

In the shadows of the outer wall, eight figures waited in hushed silence. There were still a few hours of darkness left, but the dispersing clouds in the night sky failed to block out all of the reflected light of Cerus Minor. The plain surrounding the great walled city would soon be illuminated too well to risk an open dash for freedom.

"We'll have to go now," Jason told the others. "But we're going to need a diversion."

"I could be a decoy, Commander," Lieutenant Cosgrove volunteered in a tentative voice in which bravery mingled with anxiety.

Jason had always admired the boyish officer's spunk, and knew that despite his fear, Cosgrove would willingly act as a decoy to help the others. Even if it got him killed.

"Thanks for the offer, T.R.," Jason said. "But I intend to get *all* of us out of here. Besides, I've got something else in mind." Turning to First Officer Clark, he extended his captured heat ray pistol and asked, "Do you think one of these could be jammed in some way— fixed so it won't fire until its entire power reserve has built up in the energizer chamber?"

Clark examined the weapon. "No trouble at all, sir."

"The rest of you," Jason said, "as soon as we get this set up, be ready to run." And to the girl, "Laneena—this gift of yours, what kind of range does it have?"

"By myself, I can send my thoughts halfway across the city. Why?"

"After we reach a safe distance, I want you to send out an alert. Make it sound like one of the guards reporting an attack. Do you think you can do that?"

She flashed a grin of almost wicked humor. "Just watch!"

Clark was still studying the heat ray weapon. Using the sharp edge of the outer case, he carefully probed the device. Finally finding what he sought, he scraped a wide gap in the shiny line of metallic substance that ran from one component to another. He examined his handiwork in the poor light.

"All right, Commander, I've got it," Clark said. "I've cut the control circuit that regulates the charge buildup; it's a kind of safety valve. Without that circuit, the power will build up indefinitely until it overloads. Once we trigger it, it will be a runaway reaction, and I have no idea how long we'll have to get clear."

"Is it ready to go?"

"Yes sir."

"Then take the others north along the wall." Jason took the altered weapon from him. "And don't waste any time."

"Commander—*I* should be the one to place it," Clark protested. "The risk—if I've miscalculated—"

"It was my idea. My responsibility. Now get moving!"

Clark's features showed a moment of agonized indecision, then reluctantly he started off. "Yes, sir."

Jason waited until the others were a good seven meters distant, then he placed the weapon in the open gap of a split in the wall's surface. Preparing himself, he picked up a small rock from the ground and jammed it in the gun's trigger mechanism.

And then he ran.

All of them did. Faster than they thought possible, until the sound of their pulses began to thud heavily in their ears. Jason caught up with the others as they reached a distance of one hundred meters, and still they ran. Behind them, a high-pitched whine began to increase in intensity. The heat ray pistol was overloading, building up power in a way that could only end in a destructive flare of energy.

They had reached a distance of three hundred meters along the wall when the whine reached its peak, a shrill scream almost above the range of human hearing. Abruptly, a blinding flash of light erupted behind them as the pistol detonated.

Great chunks of rock sprayed out from the shattered section of wall, undercutting the top of the wall and dropping part of the parapet to the ground with a dull *whump*. The earthmen had wanted a diversion, and they got a bigger one than they had expected. All stopped running now, some stumbling to a halt as they attempted to slow their forward momentum.

Jason said, "Laneena—send the message now!"

Heart pounding, she leaned back against the wall for support.

Eyes closed, forehead wrinkled with the effort, the girl formed the alien words in her mind. Words that would bring guards from all the nearby sections of the wall to the point where the explosion had occurred. If their plan worked. . . .

Within seconds, the sound of galloping hooves came along the parapet above them. One, two, then more of the Epos passed by them, racing to the destroyed section of wall. Jason waited a moment; then, when he was sure no more guards would pass—

"Over the top—quickly!" he ordered. "We've got to reach the edge of the forest before they realize what's happened."

Jason and Clark boosted the others to the parapet, then scaled the wall themselves. They leaped at once to the ground below, for to stay within view atop the wall for even a second longer than necessary could prove disastrous. Hugging the outer wall for the first fifty meters, the eight humans raced away from the city at an oblique angle toward the forest beyond, counting on the distraction they had created to give them time to reach it. If only the Epos did not see them!

Like silent ghosts their silhouetted forms sped across the open plain and away from the city of the Epos. Fatigue and tension conspired to slow them down, but still they pressed on. Only when they encountered the plant growth at the fringe of the forest did they slow their pace.

A burst of light came flashing from the city. Barely above their heads, a tree limb erupted into flames. So their trick had been discovered, almost too soon!

They ran on into the vegetation, striving to lose themselves in the tangled plant growth before the guard patrols were sent out from the city. They could not travel more than a few miles before dawn, but whatever distance they could gain would be helpful. Jason led the way, working through the matted growth. After two kilometers, the girl abruptly halted Jason.

"This way," she said; "we must go this way to reach the nearest travel tube."

"Travel tube?" Jason asked.

"It is the way to my village."

Jason hesitated. "I fully intend to take you there, but we should try to reach our own people first. They have weapons that will enable us to fight off the Epos."

Laneena was insistent. "No—you will never reach your people through the forest. The patrols will catch us if we stay out in the open. The travel tube will give us safety and shelter."

"All right," Jason said. "Lead the way."

They angled away from the direction they had been taking, following her as quickly as the dense growth and the darkness would permit. Another ten minutes of slow progress brought them to a familiar but unexpected sight: one of the enormous hollow vines that ran throughout the forest seemingly without termination. Laneena ran to the side of the great tube of living plant matter.

"Quickly," she said, motioning, "we must get inside."

Without questioning her, Jason drew his heat ray pistol and prepared to burn an opening in the side of the vine.

"Not that way," she said. "It will sear the tissue and make it heal more slowly."

Laneena was already stooping, reaching into her right boot where a hidden sheath held a long, thin knife. With the quick expertise of someone well accustomed to the task, she cut an opening in the vine's wall large enough to admit them, but leaving the flap of tissue connected on one side. Wiping the blade on the ground, she replaced it in her boot.

She immediately stepped inside the hollow vine, disappearing into an even greater darkness than that of the forest. The others followed, somewhat uncomfortable at the prospect, but still trusting in their newfound ally.

Here the air was cool and oddly sweet. The sounds of the forest seemed muffled and remote. When the last man was inside the vine, the girl pushed the flap of plant tissue back into place, closing the strange "door" they had made.

Jason helped her with it, pressing the flap back into line with the wall of the tubelike vine. As he did so, he could feel the sticky sap secreting from the cut edges, repairing the damage. In moments the cut would be completely healed and nearly undetectable.

Close to his side, Laneena said, "The Epos think we are primitive and helpless, like the others they enslave." A sense of pride and grim humor underlay her words. "They know less than they think."

She moved past the others to lead them and had taken a few steps within the tube when she abruptly halted. "Shhh!" she ordered. "Be quiet and don't move."

Jason was directly behind her, and although he could not see her he had the clear impression she was listening. Then he realized she was listening not with her ears but with her *mind*. At first he could hear nothing himself. But after a minute or so a faint sound began to make its way through the vine tissue.

Rhythmic hoofbeats crunched through the underbrush outside the vine tube. An Epos patrol!

Several of the creatures seemed to pause outside. Why? Had they somehow detected the resealed opening in the vine? Was their hearing so acute that they sensed the humans' presence? Jason held his breath, and knew the others were doing the same.

At last, the Epos guards moved on and the sound of the patrol grew fainter, steadily diminishing until it was altogether gone. For the moment, at least, the danger was past. Breathing easier now, Laneena resumed the journey, with Jason and the others following.

Walking inside the vine was not difficult. The spongy yet firm lining of the plant tube softened their footsteps and presented a far less hazardous path than the jungle had. They had shelter from the elements, and from the prowling beasts of night. Even in the utter darkness they had no fear of losing the path, for they were within it. They had only to touch the inner wall of the tube to guide themselves.

Along the way they occasionally encountered offshoots that connected with other vines. But Laneena invariably knew which direction to take, moving with a sureness that seemed remarkable considering the lack of visual landmarks. Or were there guideposts of a different kind? In changing from one vine to another, Jason thought he sensed a variation of the basic scent of the plant tissue. The first they had entered had smelled oddly sweet, the next faintly musty, and now this one bore the trace of an odor reminiscent of cinnamon. It was possible Laneena's people knew their way through the vine system as much by olfactory sense as by sight.

Jason walked close behind the girl, following her lead in the strange corridor. He was keenly aware of her physical nearness, the scent of her hair, the delicate brush of her hand as she called his attention to a change of direction through the vines. He was glad he had learned of her imprisonment and been able to help. He had only known her now for a matter of hours, yet already he felt drawn to her more than to any other young woman he had ever met, either as a civilian or on the Starforce vessels to which he had been assigned. Maybe it was only the situation in which they now found themselves, the danger and the common enemy. At least, that was what he told himself.

"When were you captured?" he asked her, suddenly breaking the silence.

"This morning," she said. "I left my village quite early. I had to get away for a while, to think. The forest is beautiful in the morning."

"And you ran into a patrol?"

"Yes." There was again a certain hesitancy in her voice. "My thoughts were inward and I was not paying attention."

She fell silent. Jason wondered what could have caused her to leave her village, so troubled that she failed to sense the approaching patrol. He thought of asking, but in her manner and mood he sensed a need for privacy, a need for silence and time with her own thoughts. So he did not ask. . . .

"I don't like it," Brant said as he paced around the *Eclipse*'s cargo deck. "I don't like it one bit."

"And *I* don't like being roused from my sleep at this ungodly hour," Oleg Rondell asserted. Dressed in sleeping garments and tentlike robe, he stood near the huge stack of supplies, arms folded in a pose of imperial irritation. "Especially when nothing warrants it."

"Nothing?" Flight Engineer Brant whirled on his heel. "The commander missed his transmission to us last night at dusk. We haven't had contact with them for a day and a half. You call that nothing?"

"Certainly nothing that couldn't have waited until morning. Why, there could be any number of reasons—"

"Of course there are. And none of them pleasant. I'm sure it's not a problem with their communications gear. There are backup circuits in the equipment, and Lieutenant Cosgrove took a replacement-parts kit with him in case repairs were needed."

"Even so," Rondell countered, "they may have actually *made* a transmission last night, only to have it blocked by some . . . some quirk of conditions on this accursed planet."

Brant drew in a breath and let it out slowly. "Perhaps. But if they *had* failed to reach us they would have tried again."

Zelig Farand entered the cargo deck and approached them. He was dressed in his formal business suit, but was still tugging on his jacket.

Most of the remaining crew and honor guard soldiers were also gathering in the cargo area now, bringing expeditionary equipment and supplies, and standard issue Starforce weaponry. And several of the men were beginning to set up portable force shield units and defensive systems within the gaping mouth of the cargo hatch.

Rondell watched in consternation. Turning on Brant he snapped, "Who's responsible for this? Is this your doing?"

Too weary of Rondell's petulance to care about his reaction, Brant said simply, "Yes."

"How dare you!" Rondell exploded. "You've no authority to act without my approval. *I* am in charge of this vessel."

"Were in charge," Brant corrected. "Acting under the commander's orders, issued before he left, I am now assuming command here."

"You can't. I won't allow it. I—"

Brant cut him off. "You have nothing to say about it. I have my orders. Someone has to take action."

"Action?" Rondell's outrage was giving way to worried curiosity. "What kind of action? What are you planning, Brant?"

"At first light, I'm taking ten men out in a search party to see if we can locate the others."

"Ten? You can't be serious! Add that number to those that Smith took with him, and we'll be left defenseless!"

"Hardly," Brant said brusquely. "You'll still have half the honor guard soldiers, and enough defensive gear to protect yourselves."

Rondell was not convinced. "Be reasonable. You know a good many of those remaining men are still recovering from their injuries!"

"None of them serious. I'm sure you'll be safe enough."

Rondell seemed to flounder, searching for a better argument, and Zelig Farand was ready to supply one. "If something *has* happened to the others, what makes you think you'll fare any better? You don't even know where to look for them."

Brant watched as the soldiers readied their equipment. "It shouldn't be hard to track them. We'll follow the same signal that they did. And we'll be *ready* for trouble."

Rondell sniffed with displeasure. "I can well imagine. If an alien culture *is* present on this world, it should be contacted through diplomacy, and not reckless militaristic bravado."

"Then perhaps," said Brant, "you'd like to lead this search party yourself?"

Rondell's face colored. He had walked into a trap of his own making. "Don't be absurd! That's not at all what I'm suggesting. I'm saying there should be no search party at all. At least, not yet." Recovering his composure, he made a sweeping gesture, taking in the gathered soldiers, and said in a grandiloquent tone that would have done any actor proud, "I mean, why risk the lives of these *good* men unnecessarily?"

It was such a transparent and blatant attempt to curry favor with the men that, despite his anger, Brant almost laughed out loud. But his humor faded quickly when he noticed that, with the exception of a few of the regular crewmen, the soldiers were not smiling. They were listening to the discussion with deadly seriousness, a ready audience for Rondell's cheap theatrics.

Grim-faced now, Brant said, "As I see it, the risk is about the same whether we go or stay. The matter is closed."

To the lieutenant who was overseeing the preparations, Brant said, "Keep things moving here. I'm going to give the main radio one more try."

"Right, sir."

With that, Brant left, crossing the expansive cargo area and heading back for the corridor and elevator that would convey him to the *Eclipse*'s operations deck. As soon as he was out of sight, Farand pulled Oleg Rondell aside for a conference.

"This is getting out of hand," he told the diplomat. "It was one thing giving Smith enough rope to hang himself, but if we allow Brant to further reduce the ship's security force, we could be in great danger."

"I quite agree," Rondell said. "I didn't expect he would act this soon."

"Nevertheless, he has. And there's little time for us to stop him."

"Time, yes. We need more time. But frankly, under the circumstances, I don't see what we can do."

"Just leave that to me," Farand told him.

On the operations deck, Brant was bending over the communications console as Farand entered. The businessman glanced quickly about. No one else was present here.

Brant sensed someone behind him, turned and saw Farand, then returned his attention to the open panel in the console. "If you've come here to try to talk me out of the search," he said, "you're wasting your time."

"Well, it's my time to waste, isn't it," Farand said with shallow cordiality. "Is there something wrong with the equipment?"

"No, not really. I'm just trying to use one of the backup amplification circuits to boost the signal. But I don't think it's going to work. There's just not enough power."

Farand watched as Brant's fingers probed the circuitry within the console. "How unfortunate. It might save you the trouble of an expedition." When Brant did not respond, he added, "You know, you really should reconsider your decision. Representative Rondell could make things very difficult for you back on Earth, and I'm not without influence myself. On the other hand, we could be very helpful to your career, if you demonstrated, shall we say, a certain wisdom and cooperativeness—"

"As I said," Brant told him sharply, continuing to work, "you're wasting your time."

"So it seems. But the effort had to be made."

Farand turned and took three steps away, then halted. Silently, he turned back around, his hand darting into a pocket of his suit. Producing a palm-sized weapon, he aimed it at Brant's back and fired.

There was a sharp, high-pitched whine, brief and nearly inaudible. Brant stiffened, straightening for a moment, then collapsed and fell heavily to the deck.

Quickly now, Farand moved to the flight engineer's still form. He stooped and touched Brant's neck, feeling for a pulse. He found it, although it was weak. Farand rose and pocketed the tiny nerve gun.

Stepping over to the communications console, Farand switched on the intercom circuit to the cargo deck, where virtually everyone was gathered now. He paused a moment to frame the words, then spoke in a carefully controlled tone.

"Attention—you'd better get the med tech up here at once. There's been some sort of short circuit in the radio, and Officer Brant got quite a jolt. He's unconscious now, and I'm afraid it may be serious."

Dawn brought pale-green light into the hollow of the vine. Softly filtered light that bathed the eight humans in a pleasant glow, and seemed to energize the air itself. Fatigued as they were, there was still something refreshing about the look of morning, even here on this strange world. They walked a bit faster now, glad to see once more where they were going.

"How much farther?" Jason asked. He had been hard pressed to judge distance in the meandering course of the vines. And sealed inside the tube, there was no way to tell their position in the jungle.

"We are almost there," Laneena replied. The mood of subtle despair that had hovered over her the night before was gone now. "We'll have to leave this travel tube soon, though. There's a break in the pathway between here and the village."

No more than a few minutes after she had said it, they reached a sharp bend in the hollow vine. The remarkable pathway nearly bent back upon itself, then headed off in yet another direction.

Reaching into her boot sheath, Laneena withdrew her long knife and swiftly cut an opening in the wall of the vine as she had done before. This time, Jason and the others could see the implement clearly.

Jason said, "May I see that?"

Though puzzled, the girl placed the blade in his extended hand and watched as he turned it slowly, examining it. Clark's frown of curiosity as he peered over Jason's shoulder struck her as mildly amusing. Had they never seen a knife before?

"It can't be, of course," Clark said, his eyes still fixed on the odd blade, "but I'd swear that's made of the same metal alloy they used for our early spacecraft, back when weight was still a problem."

"Just what I was thinking," Jason replied. "Yet supposedly, no Earth vessel has ever been to this world."

"Not that we know of, sir. But then, who'll know *we've* been here, unless we get back?"

"Outside, quickly," Laneena reminded them, for the wall of the vine was beginning to seal closed.

As they stepped outside the vine they were met with a startling sight. They were standing on a tiny island of solid land in the midst of a great and primitive swamp. Grayish mist hung heavily in the air about them, smelling musty and pungent.

"This way," Laneena directed. The rising slope of a fallen tree was no more than ten meters away. Halfway along its length, another tree crossed the first, supported by rough-hewn braces that at first appeared to be part of the natural surroundings.

Scaling the tree with the fluid grace of a cat, the girl advanced carefully along the crude highway in the air. Jason followed, with the others close behind him. The elevated path led for some distance into the swamp, over pools that would swallow up a man should he lose his footing.

The crude bridge angled down now, at last bringing them to ground on another small island. Moving past brush and stubby, gnarled trees, they came upon a new giant vine that began on the island and stretched out into the distance. It was virtually the same as the others encountered thus far, but it led their gaze to a sight more remarkable than any the stranded earthmen had seen.

Vines from a dozen different directions reached in across the swamp to a central point. Where they met, an enormous structure blossomed. Formed of one continuous surface of plant substance, the domed and bulging form might have been nothing more than some monstrous freak of plant growth—a quirk of nature run wild. But Jason sensed it was more than that. Far more.

It was an incredible city. . . .

CHAPTER 11

THE PLANT DWELLERS

Laneena pointed across the half-kilometer stretch of bog that lay between them and the mountainous plant growth beyond. Her flame-red hair gleamed brilliantly even in the gray mist.

"My home," she said, with an odd mixture of pride and irony. "We'll be safe now. Nothing can touch us here—not the beasts, not the Epos, nothing. Before you stands our home—the village of the race of Hoo."

The girl quickly sliced an opening in the new vine and entered. One by one, the others followed.

Spore scent filled the air of the hollow vine. The musty smell of fungus growth was much stronger here, and there was something else as well. The sound of activity, faint at first, came from ahead and grew steadily louder, attended by human voices.

Jason and the others covered the remaining distance swiftly. The hollow vine abruptly flared, the vine walls expanding into a series of enormous chambers. Sturdy ribs of plant tissue arced along the walls and rose in free standing clusters from ground to ceiling, supporting the complex dome. Something about the graceful curves of organic growth reminded Jason of the ancient cathedrals of Europe, and brought to mind such archaic terms as arches and buttresses. Only this structure was asymmetrical and free form, and had been *grown* rather than built. Eerie and strange, this village within a giant living shell of plant growth had a quality of primitive beauty.

Rising at least thirty meters into the air, the translucent vaulted chamber of the hollow plant cast a bright greenish glow over all the village. Two- and three-level buildings simply made from wood and thatching brought in from the forest lined the dirt roads. Here and there, at regular intervals along the main road, craterlike growths of the plant erupted through the soil. In these craters, water collected as in wells, but here was seeping in from the surrounding tissues of the great city-plant. The air had a sweet freshness, apparently replenished by the plant's own metabolic processes. Here was truly a balanced city environment.

A crowd was beginning to gather along the road as Laneena and the earthmen advanced into the village. They were a remarkable race of beings—totally human in appearance, yet all sharing the same characteristics as Laneena. Their skin oddly pale, each of the humans had the same striking flame-red hair.

Men, women and children were gathering now in greater numbers. All were dressed in the same green material that had the look of heavy silk. On many of their faces was joy at the sight of Laneena, and yet they held back and did not speak, plainly curious and wary. The earthmen did not fit in here, and Laneena's return with them now raised questions in their minds.

Ahead, a larger structure stood at the termination of the road. Taller than any other building in the village, it rose four stories in height. Ornate decorations on the surface of the elaborate edifice left no doubt that it was the center of power. A group of young men and women stood in casual formation at the gates, armed with gleaming knives and metal-tipped spears.

As they halted before the gates, a tall figure emerged from the building and hurried toward them with long striding steps. His green robe, trousers and boots were no more luxurious than those of the other villagers, yet in his bearing and manner, in his very *being*, was stamped the unmistakable mark of authority.

His hair and short beard were curly thickets, wildly regal, their red turning gray like a fading sunset. They framed a face that was rugged and weathered, but beneath the lines and outward signs of age there was a robust glow, an almost boyish energy. It twinkled in his alert eyes, and echoed in his walk.

"Laneena!" he said, brawny arms outstretched as he reached the girl. Embracing her fiercely, his eyes closed a long moment, his features still showing a torment only now relieved. "My God, girl, I'd thought we'd lost you."

"I'm all right, Father," Laneena said. Her voice was shallow and expressionless. The fiery self-confidence she had displayed earlier was gone now.

He stepped back a pace but still held his daughter at arm's length, his strong hands resting gently on her shoulders. "When you didn't return, we sent search parties out. They looked everywhere they could, even into the night. Then they were nearly captured by an

Epos patrol; there must have been a hundred of the enemy in the forest last night."

"They were looking for us," Laneena told him. "I was captured in the morning and taken to their city. But these men helped me escape."

The man's gaze fell upon Jason and the others, his look wary. "Did they, now?"

Laneena moved to Jason's side, remembering at last to introduce them. "This is my father, Shannon. He is the elder of our village. Father—this is Jason. If not for him and his friends, I might be on my way to the Citadel by now."

At mention of the Citadel, Shannon's face went pale. But his alert gaze remained cautious and skeptical.

Jason said, "Our escape was as much due to your daughter's abilities as to our own efforts."

"Well, then you must tell me all about it," Shannon said. He gestured toward the building behind him, even as his eyes darted to the heat ray pistols tucked into the earthmen's belts. "We offer you our hospitality. Come, let's go inside. There are many questions to be answered. But . . . leave those weapons of the Epos out here."

Jason and Danny Clark exchanged quick glances. There was no reason really to mistrust Laneena's people, and yet . . .

"Come, come," Shannon chided congenially, "we're all civilized men, aren't we?"

"Father," Laneena said, "is it necessary?"

"It's all right," Jason told them, handing over his own pistol and motioning for his men to do likewise. "We have no need for weapons, among friends."

Clark and Cosgrove handed over their ray pistols with a certain reluctance, but neither questioned their commander's decision. One of the guards at the gate gathered up the weapons and put them in a pouch.

It was a calculated risk, Jason thought, and something of a grand gesture. He hoped it wasn't also a foolish one.

The guard who now held the weapons, a young man that looked strong and muscular, brushed past Laneena as he moved to rejoin the other guards. Shannon noticed this with a frown.

"Namon," he said, "have you nothing to say to the girl you will marry?"

The one addressed as Namon abruptly halted and studied Shannon a moment. Then he turned to Laneena.

"Forgive me," Namon said. "My thoughts were elsewhere. I'm grateful you weren't hurt."

Laneena said only, "Thank you," and averted her eyes.

It was a peculiarly subdued greeting, Jason thought, for two people in love. The strangeness of it bothered him almost as much as the news that Laneena was pledged to marry. But he told himself it was none of his business, on either count.

"This way," Shannon directed them, returning through the gate toward the building.

Namon handed the pouch of weapons to one of the guards who waited at the gate, then he and the others escorted Jason and his men inside. Shannon led the way up well-worn steps of wood, taking them all to the second floor.

Light came in through tall windows that needed no glass or shutters in this strange covered village. It illuminated the building's interior with a soft, even glow that was quite pleasant, and combined with the varied smells of exotic woods and plant fibers the place had a richly primitive charm. Guards flanked a doorway to a room beyond, and it was toward this that Shannon headed.

Shannon swung open the doors and entered the room, which proved to be a large meeting hall dominated by a long wooden table with chairs arranged neatly along the sides. And at the far end of that table a larger seat was placed, unadorned and practical looking, but impressive.

"Please, be seated," Shannon said, taking his place at the end. He waited as the others took seats near him, sitting relaxed yet poised and vaguely lionlike. "Now you must tell me more about this miraculous escape of yours. How did you manage to get away?"

"The first opportunity came when I was taken to the city arena," Jason began, then quickly described the events leading to his return to the stockade and their journey to the city wall and beyond. Laneena eagerly filled in some of the gaps, explaining with returning enthusiasm how she had tricked the Epos guards with her telepathic ability. But even as they spoke, Jason noticed that Shannon was listening with almost skeptical detachment.

When Jason had finished, Shannon commented, "Remarkable. A truly bold escape! Yet you have not said how you came to be captured."

"We were traveling," Jason told him, "in the forest."

"Traveling?" Shannon said casually, perhaps a bit *too* casually. "From where?"

"Just . . . traveling. Our first camp was in a place well south of here, and our homeland is very far away."

First Officer Clark nodded in somber agreement. *"Very."*

Shannon ignored this. "South of here, you say? Then you wouldn't be Northlanders, would you now. Some of our people migrated in that direction some years back, and we've heard not a word from them since."

"North?" Lieutenant Cosgrove inquired, thinking of the mysterious signal that had first drawn them from their ship. "Did they have radio gear?"

"Radio . . . gear?" Shannon said. "I know nothing of that. But I'd like to hear more of this escape. I can't for the *life* of me understand how you could have managed it."

Jason did not like the unspoken challenge in the remark. "I think I've explained it about as well as I can . . . or care to."

Laneena also sensed the hostility in her father's words. "Why are you being rude to them? These men saved my life! They've shown me nothing but kindness since we met."

"Of that I'm sure," Shannon said with irony. "And to return that kindness, you brought them here, just as they wanted."

"It was *my* idea to bring them here," Laneena insisted. *"They* wanted to go back to their own people."

Shannon shrugged. "Or so they said."

"And I believe them," Laneena told him pointedly. "Why don't you?"

Shannon slowly rose to his feet and leaned forward with his broad hands palms down upon the table. The veneer of cordiality which had been present before now vanished. The sparring was over. "Make no mistake, girl: glad I am that you're back with us safe and sound. But your returning with these strangers is what worries me. Use that pretty head of yours! Why have *they* succeeded in escaping from the Epos when those captured from our village have failed?"

Laneena faltered, momentarily at a loss for words. Then she offered the only explanation she could think of quickly. "They . . . they are not like our people, Father."

A glint of irony flashed in Shannon's alert eyes. "There's more truth to that than you know, girl. More truth indeed!"

Angry now, Jason said, "I think you'd better explain—" and started to rise from his chair. But even as he did so, firm hands gripped his shoulders and forced him back down. A quick glance around told him that the young guards were responsible. They had quietly taken up positions behind Jason and his men during the conversation, and the sharp points of their spears were now held menacingly near.

Jason returned his gaze to the village leader and said with cold contempt, "If this is the hospitality you extend to your guests, then I wonder how you treat your enemies."

"*Father—*" Laneena said.

But Shannon waved aside his daughter's protest with a gesture for silence. "Friends or enemies," Shannon said to Jason, "we treat each as well as they deserve. But which of the two are you, now? I only know that none of our friends have the kind of weapons that you do."

Laneena could not hold back. "They have no weapons, except for what they took from the Epos."

"Took . . . or were given?" Shannon moved away from the table, his tone and expression hard and unyielding. "And I'm speaking of more than just the weapons they surrendered here. If it's proof you need, girl, it's proof you'll have."

He went to a low cabinet constructed of materials resembling bamboo and wicker that stood along one wall, raised the lid and reached inside. Withdrawing a bulky object from the dark interior of the cabinet, he closed the lid and returned to the table.

Jason and his men instantly recognized what Laneena's father held. It was a standard-issue webbing harness of the United Earth Starforce, and attached to it were a force gun, interrupter and other pieces of military equipment. Under the circumstances, he could hardly have presented more damaging evidence. And the irony of ironies was that the earthmen themselves had unwittingly supplied it!

Shannon placed the equipment before his daughter, but there was no sense of triumph in his words. If anything, his tone became more gentle. "We found these on the body of a man discovered yesterday in a travel tube well to the south. It was while our people searched for you. The man's clothes were identical to those worn by your newfound friends here, so there can be no doubt he was one of them."

Laneena was confused by the evidence facing her, but she still held an unreasoning faith in the men who had effected her rescue. "I—I don't know what these prove. What are you saying?"

"Only the Epos have weapons such as these," Shannon said, then drove the point home. "The Epos—and those humans willing to work for them."

"I can't believe that—"

"And why not? You know nothing of these men, Laneena. Why can't you accept the possibility that your miraculous escape was nothing more than a well-engineered plan? A trick. A means by which the Epos could learn the secret route to our village."

Her self-confidence returned in a fiery surge as she shot to her feet. *"No,"* she said stridently. "That's not the way it was, Father. And I'm not so great a fool that I can be tricked by just anyone who comes along. You should know me well enough by now to understand that."

Jason could remain silent no longer. "Shannon, I don't know what the laws of your village are, but in my land the accused has the right to speak in his own defense. You *do* have laws here?"

Shannon turned to study this outspoken young man who seemed not the least bit intimidated by the guards' show of force. "Oh, yes . . . we have laws. Such few as we need to ensure peace and order and fairness to all. And I'm the final arbiter in all matters of law and conduct here. So by all means go ahead and speak, and speak convincingly. If I'm wrong I'll be the first to apologize. But if I'm right," he added gravely, "you'll never leave this village."

Jason leaned forward as much as he thought he could without provoking the guards behind him. He spoke evenly and firmly, never letting his gaze waver from Shannon. "I don't deny that we had weapons such as those you found. There's no reason to deny it. But what we had were taken by the Epos when they captured us, and are still in their city. Maybe nothing I say *can* convince you. But you're making an enormous mistake if you think only the Epos have weapons more advanced than your—your stone-age spears and knives!"

"Stone-age, are we?" Shannon replied, his lips twisting in wry amusement. "Our humble weapons have served us well enough here in the forest and swamp."

"That may be," Jason told him. "But you'll never defeat the Epos with them. The best you can manage is to keep things as they are, with no hope of helping the humans in the city or of making life less dangerous for your own people."

Jason paused a moment, his mind still searching for some bit of logic to prove his case. But if there was one, which he was beginning to doubt, it still eluded him. "Look," he said at last, "I don't blame you for being cautious. I would be, too, in your position. But your mistrust is not only endangering me and my friends here, it also jeopardizes the safety of the rest of my people who are still stranded in the forest some distance from here. They're my responsibility, Shannon; surely you can understand what that kind of responsibility means. And if I have to fight you and your guards to get back to them, then I'd rather die trying than just sit here and wait for you to decide what to do with us."

Shannon had listened patiently to Jason's statement, his eyes alert and twinkling with energy, seeming to miss nothing. And now the expression on his weathered face was beginning to look less like skepticism and more like respect.

"I can see," Shannon said, "why my daughter has such unswerving faith in you. You have spirit, I'll give you that. And either you're the grandest liar I've ever seen, or you're telling the plain truth." He gestured to the guards.

Jason sensed the guards shifting their position behind him and ventured a glance around. The young villagers had stepped back and raised their spears to an upright position, removing the unspoken threat their weapons had posed. Shannon, it seemed, had decided to believe Jason. All the earthmen breathed an inward sigh of relief.

Smiling at them, and it seemed a genuine smile now, Shannon said to Jason, "You've the manner of a man used to command. That's not easily come by, especially among the humans enslaved by the Epos. I apologize for putting you through this, and I hope you can forgive me my doubts. But I *had* to be certain."

Jason got to his feet. "Then you will help us?"

"Help you?" Shannon chuckled heartily, and Jason suddenly found himself liking this man who had just minutes before seemed so menacing. "Of course we'll help you. You've saved my daughter from torture and almost certain death, and we can do no less than treat you as heroes. But if you intend to return to your people, you must wait awhile yet. The forest is still swarming with enemy patrols. The chances for safe travel will be better tomorrow. Besides," he added, "you must help us celebrate our good fortune. Namon—show our guests to my quarters and see if you can find them some clean clothes. After all they've been through, I'm sure they'll be wanting a good scrub."

Behind Shannon's dwelling was a small courtyard and garden, at one side of which stood a semienclosed structure which Jason recognized as a kind of primitive shower stall. A small wooden tank above it had been made waterproof with resin, and was fed from a well a few meters away by a chain of buckets which ran from a pulley beneath the water's surface to another pulley above a trough sloping down to the tank's open top. Namon demonstrated how to fill the tank by pulling down on the descending side of the bucket loop, and showed them the simple valve beneath the tank that would bring the water cascading down on the user. It took no small amount of effort to hoist the filled buckets to the top, making it clear that Shannon got his daily exercise and his morning's ablution at the same time.

There was an aromatic cleansing oil distilled from plant fats, and big towels of an olive-hued cloth that, though coarse and crudely woven, dried the moisture from their bodies like a sponge. And by the time all had washed, Namon returned with an armload of clean clothes borrowed from villagers eager to assist the men Shannon had called heroes.

"I once read an interesting monograph," First Officer Clark dryly observed as he finished dressing. He shifted uneasily in his rough-made garments. "The point of which was that civilization did not truly begin until the invention of underwear."

Jason smiled as he fitted his own green garments into place. Their texture against his skin was certainly a change from the nonwoven garments issued to Starforce soldiers. "Perhaps. But let's not over-look the accomplishments these people have made. Considering the living conditions on this world, I think they've done remarkably well."

Lieutenant Cosgrove was listening attentively to their conversa-tion while dressing. His slight form nearly lost in the clothes loaned him, he had to cinch up the pants cord around his waist, and roll the cuffs up so they would not drag the ground. The shirtlike robe hung down almost to his knees.

"One thing for sure," Cosgrove said, looking himself over resign-edly. "They can't be advanced enough to have any connection with that radio signal from the north. They don't even seem to know what a radio *is!*"

"How do we account for these people, Jason?" Clark said. "I mean, except for minor differences they look like us. And the lan-guage they speak is plain old Earth English, even if there is a slight dialectal twang to it."

"I can think of only one explanation," Jason told him. "It's the details that have me puzzled. . . ."

With the sun of Cerus Major high in the sky, even more light pen-etrated the walls of the great city-plant, bathing the village in a bright and cheery glow. A festival was taking shape in the wide main road, with tables from every household assembled in long lines and decorated with huge leaves and cut flowers in a myriad of colors. Some of the villagers played merry music with simple stringed in-

struments and flutes of the bamboolike reed, and all were entering
into the celebration with the enthusiasm and zest typical of a small,
cooperative community.

The meal was informal, with no speeches to interrupt the flow and
interplay of conversations, and no particular order to the serving of
foods. Rather, everyone helped himself to whatever he wished, from
platters piled high with assorted fruits and vegetables of native origin, crusty dark breads with a coarse texture and nutlike flavor,
stout bamboo pitchers of fruit beverage and wine, and chunks of
boiled meat seasoned with a spice unlike anything the men from
Earth had ever tasted.

Jason and his men sat at Shannon's table, near the end of the
great roadway. Laneena sat near her father, with her fiancé, Namon,
at her side. In stark contrast to the festive mood of everyone else,
the young couple was an island of somber quiet. Laneena poked at
her food and ate without enthusiasm.

Jason could hardly keep his eyes off her. She had seemed beautiful before and was even more so now, here in her own environment.
She had washed and changed to fresh clothes, more feminine garments than the functional robes and boots needed for the forest. The
tangles had been combed out of her hair, and amid her flame-red
tresses tiny flowers reposed, their color the vivid yellow of morning
sunlight, their fragrance the perfumed sweetness of nectar. He could
smell the scent even across the table from her.

Her eyes shifted over to his at that moment, probingly, as if she
read his thoughts. Could she? Probably not, he decided, but even so
she could hardly help but perceive his interest. Knowing this, and
seeing Namon so close at her elbow, Jason suddenly felt awkward
and out of place. And as irrational as he told himself it was, he also
felt a sense of loss.

Eyes downcast, he returned his attention to his food. Yet despite
the fact he had not eaten in over a day, he found he had little appe-
tite.

His men did not share this affliction. They devoured their meal
with gusto, pausing occasionally only to refill their cups or to inspect
the unusual appearance of some of the native vegetables.

"I'm not sure what this is," First Officer Clark said as he helped
himself to another thick slice of cooked vegetable. "But the taste is
rather like that of mushrooms, only a bit sweeter."

"Rumes are what we call them," said Shannon. "They're easy to
cultivate, and we eat a lot of them. If you're interested, I can show
you our farm."

"Yes, I think I'd like that," Clark said.

Lieutenant Cosgrove chose that moment to ask a question of his own. Still slightly in awe of Shannon and the strange village in which he now found himself, he pointed to the meat on his platter, which was his third helping. "Pardon me, sir. I was just wondering what you call this?"

"That? That's the flesh of the swampcrawler," said Shannon. "It's a kind of serpent."

"Serpent?" The boyish-looking lieutenant swallowed hard. "As in *snake?*"

Shannon nodded. "Of course, this wasn't the largest one I've seen. No more than a mere eighty feet, but still large enough to swallow a man whole. They're a devil of a beast to hunt."

"I can imagine," Cosgrove said weakly, putting his wooden eating utensils down and pushing his platter back a bit. To himself, he said softly, "I would have to ask. . . ."

Two hours later, after the celebration feast had broken up and Jason and his men enjoyed a bit of leisure time, they found themselves following Shannon on a tour of the village. Laneena and her fiancé came along as well.

Departing from the main road, they followed a winding path along lesser avenues and alleyways, moving among the villagers' huts and other buildings apparently used for storage of foodstuffs and other materials. The huts were simple affairs, constructed of rough-hewn planking fastened with either pegs or bindings of woven fibers. Though they were primarily functional, some care had been taken to make them appealing to the eye and the villagers were clearly proud of their efforts.

Because the light from the planet's sun was filtered by the plant dome's translucent walls, and no rain could reach the structures, there were virtually no effects of weathering. Also for this reason, many of the buildings lacked roofs. Those dwellings which had sleeping quarters on their second floors generally had simple roofs of planks and thatching above those sections for privacy. A few had louvered panels to admit or shut out light as desired.

"It's a simple life we live here," Shannon was telling them as they walked along. "Our daily living depends on work—on growing the food we need, on hunting, making implements, and maintaining our city and its connecting travel tubes. Our people are bound together by the common struggle to survive. Purpose and a feeling of worth bring them happiness. If not for the Epos, it could be almost ideal."

They reached the entrance to an auxiliary chamber of the great city-plant, and the scent of fungus spore grew stronger.

"This is our farm," Shannon said. "Many of the plants we eat must be brought in from the forest where they grow naturally, but those that require less light we raise here."

Surrounding them were closely spaced rows of ground vegetables, tended by men and women who had already returned to their work after the feast. Beyond them a small orchard of flowering trees bore fruit in various stages of development.

Yet this first section filled only half the chamber. In the other, a totally different food crop was being raised. The bulbous forms of fungus growth, like those Jason and his men had seen in the forest, reached high into the chamber, towering over the workers who were busily involved with the harvest of their unusual crop. The mushroomlike plants bore tops flame-red in color, balanced on thick stalks of pale orange. Some had attained a height of seven meters or more, while others were just pushing their way up through the soil.

Shannon noticed First Officer Clark's interest in these plants. "Those are the rumes of which I spoke. They grow quickly, and may be prepared in a number of ways."

"Actually," Clark observed, "I'm less fascinated with their culinary aspects than their biochemistry." Turning to Jason, he said, "It may be a cockeyed theory, but it strikes me that the similarity between the villagers' hair color and the color of these . . . *rumes* . . . might be more than coincidental."

"It makes sense," Jason agreed. "Certainly dietary influences can affect physical changes. Besides, nearly all of the humans we saw in the city of the Epos were brunets or blonds."

Shannon seemed inwardly amused at this bit of theorizing but did not comment on it. Instead he merely said, "There are also other plants that we cultivate for their medicinal properties or to use as building materials, although most of these we get from the outside."

But however extraordinary might be the village's food plants, Jason still found them overshadowed, both literally and figuratively, by the one plant they had first seen here—the one plant so vital to the village. Looking at the dome of plant tissue above them, Jason said, "You mentioned how you must work to maintain this city and the travel tubes, but you've said nothing of how they were created in the first place. Surely this isn't all a natural phenomenon?"

"Natural? Hardly!" Shannon's face crinkled with an impish grin. "Simple our weapons may be, but our skills at growing plants may just surprise you. Come—I'll show you."

With that, he led them out of the large farming chamber and through a short section of hollow vine. At the end of the tube a heavy curtain of woven fibers blocked the entrance to the next chamber. Namon held the curtain aside for the village leader and his daughter to enter, then waited while Jason and his men followed.

As they entered the chamber, a faint sound arose that was somehow familiar. In the center of the chamber stood a middle-aged man and a young woman. And throughout the rest of the area, supported on the branches of small trees, were stretched numerous vines. Vines that were swollen at regular intervals in large bulges along their length.

"We are just in time," said Shannon. "Watch this; I think you will find it interesting."

Clark exchanged a worried glance with Jason and the others, then watched intently as the man in the center of the chamber lifted an object attached to a cord around his neck, brought it to his lips and blew into it. A soft warbling sound issued from the object, a sound that seemed to stir the hanging vines with its vibrations. Suddenly, a mass of swarming, hazy things began to fill the air, drifting out menacingly. . . .

CHAPTER 12

THE BOOK OF JEN

Clark tensed, starting back a bit as the all too familiar creatures approached. But Shannon's hand stayed him.

"Don't worry," Shannon said, "these creatures are controlled, not wild like those in the forest."

As Clark continued to watch, with only minimally less concern, the pale blue puffballs with their oscillating fibers swarmed outward in circles from the vines, then moved in the direction of the strange whistle's sound. As they neared the man, he reached out and gently caught one of the furry flying creatures in his hand.

Clark winced, fully expecting the man to be painfully stung. But such was not the case. It seemed the things actually had been domesticated.

Moving forward, the young woman who stood near the man now held an earthenware container in front of him. As the man applied a slight pressure to the puffball, the creature's stinger became visible. A small amount of the poisonous venom was secreted into the container. When finished, the furry creature was released and allowed to return to the vines. The man then caught another of the puffballs, repeating the procedure, again and again until at last the earthenware crock was nearly full of the venom. As the last of the puffballs was returning to its nesting place, the girl carried the container of venom to a table laden with various items of simple equipment. The man now came forward to meet the group.

He greeted them warmly, extending his hand to each of the earthmen in turn. "The news of Laneena's safe return cheered us all."

"Jon is our master plant grower," said Shannon. "It was his grandfather who first discovered the way to control the vine growth."

The girl left the table and moved to Jon's side. Her long red hair was pulled back and braided into a thick tassel that reached to her waist. She smiled a bit less warmly than the man had, and her first glance was toward Namon rather than the strange visitors.

"My daughter, Roanne," Jon introduced her. "Yes, it was my ancestor that discovered the vine growth stimulator. The venom these creatures use is highly toxic to animal life, but on plant tissue it has the odd effect of increasing growth dramatically. After my grandfather learned how to extract the venom safely, he experimented for many months to learn how to control that growth—make it useful. Then when he had it perfected, he and my father began creating the giant plant that shelters this village."

Jason was impressed. "And you can grow the vine tubes where you want them?"

"Oh, yes. We mix other natural elements with the venom, and by injecting the mixture in one side of the vine or the other, we can control the direction of the growth."

Clark was still keeping a watchful eye on the vines even though they had become quiet, but even this concern could not suppress his scientific curiosity. "That mixture," he asked, "have you tried using it to increase the size of food plants?"

"Many times," Jon replied. "In fact, that was the original purpose of my grandfather's experiments. But sadly, some of the venom remains in the plants even after they are grown, making them unsafe to eat."

"Pity," said Clark. "That kind of growth stimulator could be a boon to agriculture everywhere, even back on—ah, our own farms."

Clark flashed an apologetic look at his commander, but saw in Jason's expression that he no longer feared revealing their background. Shannon was quick to notice this near-slip and resultant exchange of looks, and immediately seized the opportunity.

"You've yet to tell me anything of your own land," he said. Eyes twinkling, he added, "You passed our own test of trustworthiness. Have we not passed yours yet?"

Jason could not help smiling at so gentle a bit of scolding. "I'm sorry we've been secretive so far. I had my reasons, even as you had yours, but I think it's time we told you everything." Jason paused a moment, deciding how best to approach the subject. "First let me ask this," he said at last. "What do you know of Earth?"

"Earth?" Shannon abruptly sobered, then gave a disinterested shrug that was somehow not quite convincing. "Earth is no more than an old legend, barely remembered and seldom spoken of. Why do you ask?"

"Because," said Jason, "Earth is our homeland."

Shannon simply said, "I see. That would explain much." There was something of a sense of resignation—almost sadness—in his tone as he turned to Jon and his daughter and told them, "We'd best not keep you from your work. Besides, there's more I must show our visitors."

Jon nodded agreeably, but his expression was clearly one of curiosity. "We'll speak later, then." To Jason he added, "It's a pleasure to meet you all."

Shannon led the way out of the chamber, but paused at the entrance. One of his party was holding back.

"Namon," he asked, "aren't you coming with us?"

Laneena's fiancé showed a certain reluctance to answer, but finally said, "I wish to speak with Roanne. If I may."

Shannon fixed him with a questioning look, but said only, "As you wish." Turning once more, he led the others back through the vine passage that would return them to the primary chamber of the village.

He maintained an uneasy silence all the way back, a silence Jason felt unwilling to disturb. Perhaps, Jason thought, Shannon had been more troubled by their revelation than his outward calm suggested. And if that were so, it would be unwise to press the matter. Better to let things proceed at their own pace, and give Shannon time to adjust to the idea. As they walked, Laneena fell into step alongside of Jason, her long legs striding easily, her shoulder nearly touching his. The natural swing of their arms caused her hand to brush his more than once, yet she seemed not to react to it or to consider moving away. Jason half wished she had remained behind with Namon. Her nearness was becoming as painful as it was pleasant, and it was pleasant in the extreme.

Shannon's destination lay beyond the tall government building in which their initial confrontation had taken place, and took them down a long path winding its way through a well-cared-for garden. The path ended at the far wall of the great plant dome, stopping at a point where the wall's smooth surface swelled out into yet another travel tube.

Shannon said as they reached the entrance, "I'm taking you to the temple of our ancestors. Perhaps the answers we both seek are there."

The travel tube continued on for a hundred meters, twisting and turning as it meandered through the swamp that lay beyond its translucent walls. Then the vine abruptly opened into a new chamber roughly a third the size of the primary dome. The sounds of the village did not reach this spot, and both Shannon and his daughter showed a certain reverence for the area.

Hundreds of crude wooden markers were in the ground, bearing names and symbols. Some of them looked far older than others, showing signs of weathering that indicated that this area had not always been protected by the all encompassing dome of plant tissue.

Much of the chamber was clearly a burial place for the village, a cemetery for past generations. But what commanded the most attention, what riveted the gaze of the earthmen at once, was what Shannon referred to as "the temple."

The long object, tarnished in spots but still gleaming, dominated the far end of the chamber, its sleek delta wings flat against the ground. The corpulent fuselage of the ancient craft sat low and hulking, as if it had taken root in the fertile soil of Cerus Major. The ship was easily large enough to carry several hundred passengers, and on its aft fin, fading but still recognizable, was the insignia of the United Earth Space Exploration Command.

First Officer Clark was the first to speak. "Either I've gone daft, or that's a colonizer shuttle. And a very old one at that."

"I know." Jason gazed appreciatively at the craft. "That series hasn't been in use for well over a century."

Images came to mind, from lessons learned at the Starforce Academy. The shuttles were strictly landing craft, not capable of star flight, and were ferried to their destination on a central core vessel containing the living quarters and other facilities used during the flight. The composite vessel was propelled by a stardrive engine, a crude faster-than-light drive developed when mankind was still on the threshold of cooperative space exploration. Primitive by modern standards, it had still reduced years-long trips to a matter of months. It had made possible the colonization of a dozen worlds, and placed outposts on numerous others.

"Come," Shannon said, motioning them on. With his daughter now following close behind him, they entered the ship through an open hatch nearly level with the ground.

Light streamed through rows of portholes along the sides, softly illuminating row upon row of seats. The seats ran not only along both sides of the central aisle, but also in a second tier above them in the high cabin, accessible by grillwork catwalks and steps that seemed lacelike and ethereal. The seats themselves mirrored this look, their fabric covers long ago worn or rotted away to leave the bare bones of their frameworks, functional and airy. Adding to this, the polyplex panes of the portholes had become clouded and discolored, softening the light and tinting it with assorted pastel hues. It was perhaps this faint suggestion of stained-glass windows that gave the place its atmosphere—its look of churchly beauty.

"Our religious services," said Shannon, "are normally held in the village, but now and again, as the need moves us, we return here to this place of our ancestors."

At the front of the passenger compartment stood a simple altar, formed by a long panel of polyplex laid across two supplies cannisters. At the altar's center was a six-pointed cross and circle, the interfaith religious symbol that had been popular with Starforce personnel and colonizers for the past two centuries. Flanking it on either side were ancient-looking pressure helmets, and resting before it on the age-clouded polyplex surface was a metal-clad logbook. It was to this last object that Shannon went, picking it up and holding it for a long moment before finally extending it to Jason with both hands.

"Of written history, we've nothing more than this," Shannon told him. "The Book of Jen. My father taught me to read it, and his father taught him. It's a skill that's been kept in the family all these many years, even though no one else in the village bothers to learn. There's little enough need for it, the way we live."

First Officer Clark stepped forward to offer a comment. "There should have been more than that, Jason. I mean, the computer log . . . the microfilm records . . ."

"Maybe so, but either one required power to operate. Even if they were able to use the recharging units, the ship's batteries wouldn't have lasted more than a few years."

"True enough," Clark said. "None of the colonies were intended to operate without resupply from Earth. And I suppose the people here had their hands full just getting by without worrying about keeping up their history lessons."

Jason examined the book. It was a standard personal log of the type used by most spacecraft commanders. On the metal cover were etched the letters *J E N*. A look inside confirmed his suspicion that they were the initials of the ancient ship's commander.

"John Edward Nelson," Jason read aloud. "He was one of the early colonizers. According to this, his group was headed for Darros to establish a base and settlement."

"Nelson?" Clark said musingly. "Yes—I recall now. When I was a tyke I read everything I could on the early colonization program. Nelson's attempt to reach Darros was listed as a failure—the ship and all hands destroyed."

Jason continued flipping through the pages of the book, grateful that the permapaper had held up so well. He quickly scanned the lines of Nelson's writing, sensing something of the man's character in the bold yet precise script.

"They almost were destroyed," Jason said. "This says that their reactors malfunctioned and went critical. They had to brake to sublight speed and jettison the reactor pods and main drive engine to avoid the explosion. After that all they could do was drift with the momentum they had. There was barely enough emergency power for their life-support systems, and no way to transmit a message back to Earth."

"A lot like our predicament," Clark observed. "But how did they get here? This planet's at quite a tangent to the line between Earth and Darros."

"That's the odd part," Jason said, frowning in thought. "According to this, they couldn't explain it themselves. Without any discernible reason, the ship suddenly deviated from its previous course, drifting for another two months. They were almost at the end of their provisions when they became caught in the gravitational field of Dromii and were pulled into the orbit of this planet. They abandoned the core ship and reached the planet's surface in their landing shuttles."

"Shuttles?" Clark said. "Plural?"

"Yes—three in all. They lost track of one on the trip down, but this one landed here, and another landed on a plain not far from a great abandoned city—presumably the one where the Epos now rule, although it doesn't mention them."

Shannon said, "The Epos weren't here then. They first arrived when I was still a lad. Before that, a free settlement flourished in the old city. But the Epos put a stop to that!"

"Apparently there were opposing factions," Jason said, reading further. "Some of the colonists chose to live in the swamp despite its dangers, because of the abundance of food. The others chose the old city." Jason pointed his finger to a passage in the middle of the book. "This explains the name these people have for themselves. It's the last entry in the log."

The writing was still legible:

There is do doubt we shall be here for all time. Our tools, our technology, all the advantages of our civilization are lost. Even

*our cultural ways of the past must be altered for the sake of
survival on this hostile world. For survival is essential. There is
no hope of rescue, no hope of return to Earth. Yet for reasons
which cannot begin to be expressed, even here the human race
must be preserved. . . .*

In the last line, the word *human* was marred by a worn spot in the
paper, leaving only the word *hu*. By a simple mistake in reading, a
generation or more past, the "race of Hoo" had its origin.

"Look at the date," Clark pointed out. "These people have been
on this world one hundred and fifty-four years."

Jason nodded. "Long enough under these conditions to forget
where their ancestors came from, obviously. What are we talking
about—six, maybe seven generations?" He flipped back to the front
of the book. "And here's a list of the colonizers. Second in command of the mission was a man named Richard Shannon, an Irish
scientist with a background in genetics and cultural anthropology."

"My great-great-grandfather," Shannon offered. "Our legends say
that he took over after the leader of our people was killed by one of
the beasts of the forest. He brought order to our way of life, and
helped our people survive. Since then, a Shannon has always sat at
the head of the Council of Elders." He regarded Jason with a look
as troubled as it was curious. "The book has meaning for you, then?
Though we've learned the words, many of them make little sense to
us."

"It has meaning," Jason said, closing the book and returning it to
Shannon. "Your ancestors embarked on a journey long ago, leaving
Earth in a great vessel of which this—*temple*—was a part."

"Then," Shannon interrupted, "it's true the legends are? This
place we use for worship fell from the sky? Our people really came
from another world beyond the stars?"

"It's true," Jason told him. "We left Earth ourselves only a few
days ago."

A bit of Shannon's old skepticism returned. "A few days? But the
Book of Jen says our ancestors traveled for many months."

While Jason and Danny Clark considered how they might go
about explaining hyperspace, Lieutenant Cosgrove came to their rescue. "We, ah . . . we sort of took a shortcut."

Laneena then asked the question that had been on Shannon's
mind since the first mention of the word *Earth,* and perhaps subcon-
sciously since he had first set eyes upon them.

"Is that why you're here? To rescue our people . . . to take them
away, back to Earth?"

Jason shook his head. "What I said before was true: we didn't even know you were here until our own vessel crashed here. And now we're stranded, just as your ancestors were."

Shannon was clearly relieved by the news. He took the book back to its place on the altar and gently laid it down. "It's better, I think, if we do stay here. Whatever wonders Earth may have, it is still a place unknown to us. This is our home, and it's a good life we have —simple and direct and satisfying. I for one would not wish to exchange it." Turning suddenly to Jason once more, he added, "You know, of course, you're all welcome to stay here—make yourselves a part of our village."

"I'm sure I'd like that. But for now I can't say for sure what we'll be doing. I still have to reestablish contact with the rest of my people, and if there's any way I can get them safely back to Earth, that's still my responsibility."

Shannon nodded, his expression one of respect. "I understand. In the morning, we'll help you reach your friends. The Epos' patrols should have thinned out by then."

"I'm grateful for your help."

"You know," First Officer Clark observed suddenly, "it strikes me as rather an odd coincidence that two ships from Earth would malfunction in such a way as to bring them here, even this many years apart."

"I know," said Jason. "And don't forget the Epos. They *could* be native to this world, I suppose, but I've a feeling they're not. They don't quite seem to fit. And if they've come here as we have, then we have to consider the possibility that something on this world is responsible for it all."

"Some planetary phenomenon, you mean?"

"That," he said soberly, "or else deliberate manipulation on someone's part."

"A fascinating thought," said Clark. "But I daresay no one we've seen here yet is capable of anything that fancy."

"There's a lot we *haven't* seen yet."

"True. And there's still our mysterious radio signal to explain."

"I haven't forgotten that for a moment. I'm convinced it's tied in with all this somehow. And whether we leave this planet or stay, that's *one* mystery I intend to solve."

CHAPTER 13

AMONG THE MISSING

Darkness reigned over the village.

The blazing orb of Dromii had set hours ago, and even though Cerus Minor was rising in the night sky, virtually none of its soft glow filtered through the great domed wall of the city-plant. No light burned in any of the homes along the main roadway or the numerous narrow avenues that crossed it. The villagers used candles after dark, made from the waxy root of a common ground plant, but the last of these had been extinguished nearly an hour ago.

Only in the garden behind the large government building did a few of the crude lamps still burn, their pale light illuminating the three earthmen who had gathered there. The four honor guard soldiers had already settled down for the night in improvised sleeping quarters within the building, but Jason, First Officer Clark and Lieutenant Cosgrove remained awake.

"Picking up anything at all, sir?" Clark asked softly.

Jason continued working the small comset, alternately sending a hailing signal on the *Eclipse*'s open frequency and then listening for a reply. The small device was among the equipment carried by the dead soldier found and buried by the villagers. The fact that Jason had neglected to order the man's weapons and gear taken along when they left his body in the hollow vine had proven a blessing. Jason tried the signal once more, listened again as only silence came back through the comset's audio circuits, then switched it off.

"No," he said at last. "Nothing. Either this unit's broken or the signal's too weak to reach the ship from here." There were other possibilities, he knew—some of which he did not care to think about. "I guess we'll just have to wait until tomorrow to find out how they're getting along."

"You know, Commander," Cosgrove said at that moment, in his

almost boyishly high voice, "if it *does* turn out that we're stuck on this planet, we could really help these people. With the weapons and other hardware we've got, we could change the balance of power here. We could force the Epos to stop their patrols—maybe even free the people in the city. We could bring the villagers up to date."

"We could," said Jason, "up to a point. But keep in mind that the colonists weren't exactly devoid of science when they landed here themselves. We're in the same dilemma they were. Hardware breaks down in time, and once the replacement parts are used up, that's it. Most of our gear is made by such sophisticated means we couldn't begin to make new parts. How do you build a microcircuit with hand tools? And as far as the Epos are concerned, with only a limited supply of force-gun pellets, we could *start* a good fight but we couldn't *finish* it."

Cosgrove sighed deeply as he realized the truth in Jason's words. "It's amazing how fragile technology is."

"Anyway," said Clark, "I wouldn't be too quick to change these villagers. If they're not interested in being taken to Earth, I rather doubt they'd care to have it brought to them. And they've improvised such an intriguing society . . . an odd amalgam of medieval European and American Indian cultures. I'd really like to study it if I have the chance."

Jason was about to tell him just how likely that chance would be when he caught sight of Laneena. He didn't know whether she had been standing there long or had just reached them.

"Laneena? You're up late."

"As are you," she countered. "I couldn't sleep."

As she stepped closer to Jason and glanced quickly at the other two men, there was something in her manner that suggested she wished to speak privately with him. Clark noticed this. He was no fool, and had been aware for some time that Jason felt drawn to the young woman. The question was, under the circumstances as they now knew them to be, would his commander prefer to be left alone with Namon's fiancée or would he rather have the company of his men to keep the conversation from getting too personal? After a moment's indecision, Clark decided to give them their privacy.

He cleared his throat. "Well . . . it's about time I turned in. How about you, Lieutenant?"

"What?" Cosgrove gave a puzzled expression at the sudden decision to retire, then under the pressure of Clark's forceful gaze caught on. "Oh . . . right. It is pretty late at that, I guess."

"If you'll excuse us, Commander," Clark said, then headed off toward the building. Cosgrove followed, with an occasional backward glance.

Laneena could not help but smile at their ill-disguised effort to cooperate. She was no fool either. But her smile faded as she turned her attention once more upon Jason. She studied him a moment in silence, sensing his fatigue.

"They're right, you know," she said. "You ought to get some rest yourself. From what you've told me, you haven't had more than a few hours' sleep in the last three days."

"Too much to think about," he answered. He found himself wondering again if she could read his thoughts as easily as those of the Epos. He hoped not. It was hard enough to guard his spoken words. He busied himself with another small device, also from the dead soldier's gear. Suddenly gesturing toward the south, he said, "My ship's out there, about fifteen kilometers away."

"How do you know the distance?"

"This tells me." He handed her the device. On its flat surface, a glowing arrow pointed south. Below that, a digital readout gave the distance, pulsing in time with a faint beeping tone. "It's an emergency tracker, used to locate a spacecraft if you're lost. It receives the ship's homing beacon. We all carry one. Or at least, we did."

Laneena held the device carefully in both hands, as if it were a living creature. She studied it, her long lashes obscuring her eyes.

"You'll be leaving in the morning," she said, and it was not so much a question as a statement.

"At dawn. We should be able to reach the ship in a few hours, using the travel tubes. Your father is sending Namon and two other men to guide us."

"Namon's a good man," she said, handing the tracker back to Jason. "The best hunter in our village. You can count on him to help you."

"So your father told me." Jason found himself staring at her, studying the way the flickering candlelight played softly over her features. "He also told me that you and Namon will be taking his place someday, as leader of the village."

"Yes . . . someday." Her look became troubled. "The people expect it, just as they expect Namon and I to marry."

"You sound . . . as if you don't want to be leader."

"I don't, really. I have enough trouble making my own decisions lately. How can I be expected to make them for everyone else?"

"I thought you did pretty well when you helped us escape."

She smiled faintly. "Perhaps you bring out the best in me." She

turned at a slight angle to Jason and began slowly pacing in a small
semicircle around him. "I don't know—sometimes I feel I don't belong here. I guess I've always felt that way."

Jason nodded in understanding. "There have been a lot of times
in my life when I've felt like an outsider myself."

"Maybe that's why you're easy to talk to," she said. "Not like
some of the young men of the village. They used to think I was cold
and indifferent . . . too proud to return their interest. Maybe I was.
But it wasn't really that I didn't like them . . . just that they didn't
understand the way I think, or feel about things. They weren't right
for me."

"And Namon is?"

Her eyes shifted up to his briefly before becoming downcast again,
and she seemed to sigh inwardly. "No . . . not really. Certainly no
more than the rest. But there's no one else in the village who would
be better. And Father likes him."

"Then . . . you don't love him?"

"Namon? No!" She laughed abruptly, an empty sound devoid of
humor. "That's not the worst of it. The feeling is mutual. He's far
more interested in Jon's daughter, Roanne, than in me."

"Then," said Jason, "I don't understand. Why the marriage?"

"As I said, it is expected of us. *I* am the daughter of Shannon the
Elder, blood heir of the family of leadership. And Namon is the
strongest and smartest and bravest young man of our village. It's
inevitable. It is said that my ancestor placed great faith in the science of pairing, and I can do no less for our people than accept the
best that is available." She paused for a moment. "Besides, my father is, as he's so fond of telling me these days, not getting any
younger. Grandchildren will please him immensely. He's already
considering names for them, and is eager to teach them their herit-
age."

Jason digested this information, more uncertain of his own feelings and priorities now than ever before. Certainly he had learned
that in ancient Europe there had been marriages of convenience—
some even involving what could only be called selective breeding.
But such a concept seemed to belong to the dim recesses of the past.
Regardless of this, did he have a right to speak out? The villagers'
cultural ways were valid to them, he realized, whether he agreed
with them or not. And he suspected any meddling on his part would
be prompted more by purely personal reasons than by altruism.

At last he said, "Have you spoken with your father—tried to explain?"

"No," she said quickly. "I couldn't hurt him. And Namon has too much respect for him to defy his wishes." She stopped her pacing, very close to him. Her eyes sought his fiercely now, no longer avoiding contact. "If you *are* able to return to Earth, do you think you'll ever come back here?"

"I don't know. My life's not entirely my own, either. If I stay in the Starforce, my orders may not permit me to return. Especially if I'm blamed for our crash landing here." He paused, assessing the effect of his words on the girl. "But unless there's a miracle of some kind, I doubt we will be leaving. I may have to accept your father's invitation to stay here."

Conflicting emotions played across Laneena's features, moisture welling up in her eyes. "Even that," she said, "will be hard."

Jason reached out to touch her cheek where a tear trickled down, and the contact triggered something within her. Impulsively, she kissed him, then buried her face against his shoulder. Her hair was soft against his face. The tiny golden flowers were gone now, but their perfume lingered. The few seconds that she stayed there seemed an eternity, and yet although he wanted to return her embrace something made him hesitate. A hesitation she seemed to sense.

She pulled away abruptly, eyes large and troubled, blotting at her tears with an awkward sweep of her hand. Her face froze into an implacable mask, and she blurted out, "Sorry—I shouldn't have—"

In the next instant she was gone, darting away from him and leaving the garden. Leaving him alone. Alone to curse whatever fate it was that forever haunted him, bringing him into situations where the timing was always wrong.

Too late . . .

As he stood there, a dozen or so meters away other eyes observed. Standing in the shadowed doorway of his quarters, Shannon watched his daughter's tearful departure from the solitary earthman. Watched, and frowned in thought.

In a realm almost beyond the imagination's ability to conceive, activities went on as they always did. Unlike that part of Cerus Major where Jason and his men were, it was not night here. In fact, it was *never* night here.

The two aliens who had been studying the activities of Jason and the others for hours upon end now turned away from the large viewing crystal, which still held the image of the plant dwellers' village.

Shom said, "What do you think now of our newest candidate? Has your enthusiasm yet given way to doubt?"

"Doubt? Not in the least!" Klon's sense of conviction was every bit as strong as earlier, if not more so. "The more I see of this human, the more I am convinced he is right for our purpose. I like the way he has dealt with the humans who live in the swampland. He shows respect for their ways. And his two friends display the same qualities. I like them all."

As they traversed the main aisle of Primary Scanning Center, moving past row upon row of viewing crystals watched by others like themselves, their steps were smooth and unhurried. Their long and glittering robes skimmed the surface of the flooring, and in the comparative darkness of the chamber the aliens still had their peculiar quality of unreal illumination.

"This one called Jason," Shom said after a moment. "Already he suspects their landing on the planet indicates, as he puts it, manipulation. Even though correct, that is still an astonishing deduction to make with such little evidence, and such small knowledge of the energies required. A creature of pure logic would not arrive at such a conclusion so readily."

"A creature of pure logic," said Klon, "would be of little use to us. Here, we have logic in abundance. It is precisely this human tendency to 'play hunches,' as they call it, to make great leaps of thought, that makes them valuable to us. They have a marvelous impetuosity."

"That same impetuosity has been at the root of much of their troubles over the centuries," Shom reminded him.

Klon shrugged it off. "Be that as it may, I still think they are exactly what we need. Besides, this Jason has already sworn to locate the source of our beacon signal."

"Yes. And I believe he will try, if he has a chance to. But even if he does, his response to what he finds there will be the telling factor, my friend. The telling factor, indeed. . . ."

The sun of Cerus Major was rising above the swamp and surrounding forest lands. Shielded from its rays, the ten men had worked their way swiftly through the system of hollow vines leading from the village to that part of the forest where the crippled Earth vessel lay waiting. More than an hour had passed since dawn, when they began their journey.

Namon and two others from the village led the way, having used Jason's information from the emergency tracker to pinpoint the approximate location of the *Eclipse* and then plot the closest route by means of the travel tubes. Part of the journey would still have to be made outside of the hollow vines, but they had stayed within the tubes as long as possible, taking full advantage of their safety and ease of progress. Jason and his men wore their uniforms once more, clean now, and felt more at ease in their accustomed garments than those borrowed from the villagers.

They walked on in silence another few minutes, then Jason indicated the emergency tracker in his hand. "We must be getting close. The signal is much stronger now, and steady."

Namon studied the direction in which the device was pointing. His gray eyes gazed ahead as he recalled the various passages they might take. "We shall have to leave the travel tube now," he said finally. "There is no other path in that direction."

"Very well." Jason fastened the tracker to the webbing harness he wore, salvaged from the dead soldier's equipment. "But let's stay alert. For all we know, there still may be Epos patrols out looking for us."

Namon pulled his alloy cutter from its sheath and sliced an opening in the wall of the vine. Brilliant sunlight flooded in as one by one the men exited the tube.

Now it was Jason's turn to lead the way. Occasionally checking the emergency tracker, he moved out in the direction of the *Eclipse,* cutting a path through the foliage with the salvaged interrupter. The force gun and pellet pods were adhered to his webbing harness, and the two captured heat ray weapons were in the able hands of First Officer Clark and Lieutenant Cosgrove.

The three village men had their own gear—knives and metal-tipped spears, odd shields of some barklike material and blowguns with poison-tipped darts. The villagers had given shields and knives to the four honor guard soldiers to offer them some protection as well, but still and all the group had only the three advanced weapons to use for anything requiring real range and power. *Three*—for ten men.

Scarcely had they covered more than a kilometer when they came upon a startling sight. Startling and unpleasant. Just twenty meters from the path they were making, the carcass of a gigantic insect lay amid the vegetation. What had killed it was hard to tell, but judging from the fact that it had not been dead long, and the fact that two dozen or more identical creatures were grazing on nearby foliage, it seemed a predator could be ruled out. Colored an earthy orange with streaks of rust brown running back along their length, the creatures had long unsegmented bodies that appeared rigid. The living creatures bore eight legs, the rear four of which were powerful-looking thrusting legs somewhat like those of grasshoppers. Great translucent wings lay folded back above the torso, golden and glittering, yet it seemed incredible that the creatures could fly. For each of them was at least six meters in length, and nearly two meters in diameter!

"Chewdevils," said Namon. "Just plant eaters. They used to be a danger to our travel tubes until we found a way to make the plant tissue distasteful."

First Officer Clark gestured toward the now limbless torso. "Looks like something's been at it."

Namon pointed to an opening in the side of the carcass's hard chitin exoskeleton. "Vulture bugs."

The others looked, not seeing at first. Then they became aware of smaller insect forms, shaped like teacups turned upside down, moving on countless tiny legs. A large number of these shiny black insects were pouring into the carcass, and an equally large number were pouring out, bloated with the soft inner tissues cleaned from the shell.

Jason made a mental note of the scene and pressed on through the forest. They could waste no more time in returning to the ship. Not a minute could be lost in rejoining the others, warning them of the Epos, and rearming themselves.

After another kilometer had been covered, the terrain began to resemble more closely that of the area where the *Eclipse* had crashed. Jason was sure they were getting closer. The emergency tracker confirmed the fact. They might even be within sight of the gleaming craft if not for the dense vegetation.

A guttural scream tore through the minor sounds of the forest. It was a familiar sound, and it froze the men in their tracks.

"Commander—" Clark snapped.

"I know," said Jason. "No sense getting in a standard defensive position without our gear. We'll just have to hope the heat ray pistols have more of an effect than our force guns did."

Crashing sounds came through the forest, coming nearer. In another moment the thing tore through the foliage in front of them. Its green fibers bristled, and its solitary eye gazed out upon the area where the men stood. Singed patches marred the red-striped torso. It was one of the same beasts Jason and his men had encountered earlier.

Clark raised his heat ray pistol as the creature began to stare in their direction. He was abruptly stopped by Namon.

"It is a *mordo*," Namon said quickly. "I have seen the Epos use their fire weapons on others like it. They can withstand much of the heat. It's no good fighting them."

"All right," Clark said. "What's the alternative?"

"This way." Namon led them off to one side. "Keep moving, don't stop. The mordo is slow to see. If we do not stay in one place too long, it will not know where we are. Only old and sick animals are captured by it."

"And ignorant spacemen," Clark said under his breath, as he realized that the so-called defensive pattern they had used before had actually made it easier for the beasts to find them.

As they moved away, the beast still kept its eye trained upon the area where they had been, the nerve impulses from its great eye filtering but slowly into its limited brain. The men moved as quietly as they could, and thankfully the varied sounds of the forest covered what little noise their progress made.

As they left it well behind and were able to return to the true course, fresh energy seemed to drive them on even harder through the matted vegetation. They knew they had to be getting close. A quarter kilometer more of terrain passed beneath their feet, and then—

"There!" Lieutenant Cosgrove said with sudden excitement. "The ship!"

His exhilaration was shared by the others. There ahead of them, the great round hull of the *Eclipse* lay silently waiting in the shadows of the giant plants.

Namon gazed up at the mammoth ship in open amazement. "It— it's nothing like the temple of our ancestors."

Clark told him, "We've had a century and a half to make improvements. But the purpose is still the same."

They wasted no time in reaching the ship, nearly running over the uneven ground. But even before they got there they could tell something was wrong. The massive hatch platform was still open as it had been, but now the boarding ladder reached down to the ground, and there was no movement visible within the spacious cargo bay. Jason called out to anyone who might be within, or nearby in the forest. No sound returned. He called again.

Silence.

"Commander—" Lieutenant Cosgrove said, motioning to the ground beneath the hatch platform. "Bad news."

Jason moved to his side and looked down at the marks in an exposed area of soil. Distinct hoofprints could be seen.

"The Epos," Jason said. "A patrol must have found the ship."

"Tracks look to be a day old, sir," Cosgrove said. He shook his head in hopeless consternation. "Brant and the others—they had weapons . . . the ship's defenses . . . How could they be overcome?"

"The same way we were. It wouldn't have been all that hard for the Epos." Beneath Jason's controlled features, violent emotions raged. "It must have happened while we were in the village. If we had just reached the ship sooner—"

"It couldn't be helped, sir."

"Come on," Jason said, scaling the ladder. The others were close behind him as he reached the hatch platform. His weapon ready, he entered the ship. He could not be sure if the Epos had left behind a guard of their own. It seemed unlikely, but then everything on this accursed planet seemed unlikely.

As they stepped into the cargo bay, the pile of containers loomed before them. "Our supplies," Cosgrove said. "But what are they doing here like this?"

"Rondell's doing, I'll wager," Clark responded. "Looks like the guards' weapons and ammo are missing. Do you think the Epos might have left the injured here?"

"I hope not." Jason headed for the passageway. "I doubt they would have left them alive."

They took the elevator up to the command center. It was empty. A check of the remaining compartments revealed the same thing: everyone left behind was now gone.

"No sign of a struggle," Jason said as everyone gathered in the corridor. "The monkeys must have drugged the guards and slipped aboard while the Epos waited outside, controlling the whole thing."

Namon still looked uneasily about the smooth interior of the great ship. "What will you do now?"

"If the men are still alive," said Jason, "then there's a chance we can rescue them."

First Officer Clark patted the heat ray pistol in his belt. "We'll need more weapons than these."

Jason considered a moment. "Maybe they didn't find the weapons locker. Let's check it out."

With a swiftness borne of desperation, they returned to the spacious cargo bay of the great cruiser. Except for the food stores and related supplies stacked neatly in the center, the cargo area was virtually empty. There were only a few crates of Earth's merchandise and materials, samples to show in the negotiations with the rulers and businessmen of Betalon. That mission seemed remote and unreal now.

Clark reached the spot first. "The panel hasn't been touched, Commander."

An inner wall of the ship flared out at an angle, forming a sloped enclosure. There were no distinguishing features to indicate that it was a storage compartment of any kind.

Jason moved to the panel and examined it for a moment, then he placed his hand on the smooth polyceramic surface and waited. Instantly, a glowing outline framed his hand as the security circuits identified his dermaprint. Then a series of glowing patterns appeared above the area where his hand rested. He touched the first, then the third pattern. The lights winked out, making the panel again appear normal.

Jason stepped back as hidden motors caused the panel to swing up and out of the way, revealing what was stored behind it. The standard complement of weapons and equipment was neatly organized there, enough for the entire crew and passengers as well. This store of gear was for emergency use, and was separate from the individual gear the men had kept in their compartments.

Now everyone, including the villagers, donned a new webbing harness, loaded it with equipment and slung extra strings of force-pellet pods over their shoulders. The remainder of the gear was placed in an equipment case which two of the men could carry with relative ease.

Jason adjusted the fasteners on his harness. His eyes roamed the interior of the cargo hold, finally settling on a storage rack on the far wall. "Danny—you and T.R. grab those cargo lifters. I think we might use them."

Clark was through with his harness adjustments first and reached the lifters before Cosgrove. The cargo lifters were broad belts of electromesh, connected to small control devices. When fastened around cargo, the antigrav force of the lifters nullified the weight of the bulky crates and let them float freely for easy movement in and out of the hold. With enough of them, they might have been able to move the ship's dislodged trans-space engine back into position, but what they had would nullify barely a third of that engine's enormous weight.

Jason said, "Namon, will your people help us rescue the others?"

The young villager did not hesitate. "Yes. Shannon will have to approve, of course, but I'm sure he will."

"Let's go back to the village, then. There's nothing to be gained by staying here, and the Epos may come back."

They left the *Eclipse* and started back for the village. Their progress was faster now, with a path already cut through the forest, and they covered ground quickly. Back past the giant insect carcass, and through the area where they had sighted the mordo. The beast was nowhere to be seen now, fortunately, apparently having given up on its elusive prey.

Another hour passed. They had almost reached the nearest branch of the travel tube system. It was partially in view, less than twenty meters ahead. In a few minutes more they could reach the relative safety of the hollow vine.

Then it happened!

A searing beam of light shot between the men, scorching the back edge of Clark's webbing harness and incinerating the foliage beyond them. Another ray flashed an instant after the first, wounding one of the honor guard soldiers in the arm.

"Epos patrol!" Jason shouted commandingly. "Defensive position —now!"

Instantly, the soldiers responded, forming the standard ring pattern. Namon and the other two villagers hesitated at first, uncertain about the safety of this new technique, then they too joined the circle. At Jason's command, they all activated the disk-shaped devices attached to their webbing harnesses. In a flash the energy fields from all their units linked, forming a complete wall of protective energy around and above them. But how well it would fare against the Epos' powerful heat rays remained to be seen.

Thirty-five meters away, the Epos patrol appeared, advancing in an area of light foliage. There were a dozen of the horse-and-monkey symbiotic teams, and as some of the Epos had more than one tiny mind slave, there were easily fifteen weapons pointed at the humans.

Each of these steeds wore an extra covering in addition to the one usually worn. Looking like some bizarre form of battle armor, the covers seemed made of asbestoslike material with an outer surface of mirror-finished metal. Each covered most of its wearer, with a wide skirt reaching down almost to the knees and separate pieces shielding the neck and head. The monkeys sat within high-rimmed shields of the same material, rising like metallic craters from the surface of the armor.

"They know we've got some of their weapons," said Jason, "and came dressed for a fight."

"It would appear so," Clark agreed. "But if we're the first humans to use heat rays against them, where'd they get the bloody armor? Doesn't look like something they whipped up overnight."

"They must have other enemies," Jason said. "Maybe their own kind."

At that moment the patrol abruptly halted their advance, still a good twenty-five meters away. Unexpectedly there came a harsh rasp of sound, metallic and grating. It quickly modulated itself into a voice, full of authority and power.

"Put down your weapons," the voice said, raw and unreal in the natural splendor of the forest. *"Surrender yourselves at once."*

Jason saw the source of the metallic command. One of the steeds wore a thick medallion about its neck, nearly identical to the one he had seen Old Stod wear back at the arena. Knowing they were dealing with something more than either the slaves of the city or the swamp people, they had come prepared for verbal communications. And now they expected Jason and his men to simply give up.

"I think not," Jason said. "Once, when we were unarmed. But not again."

When the earthmen did not respond as ordered, the Epos' leader bristled with barely concealed rage. To have his authority and power challenged by these sub-Epos creatures was intolerable. He cantered forward a few paces, neck arched stiffly and eyes flared wide in anger. As more mental commands triggered the circuits within the medallion around his neck, the artificial voice blared out, "If some of you must die to convince you, then I will start with those from the swamp."

With that, the patrol leader's tiny mind slaves jerked erect and fired their heat ray pistols directly at Namon and his friends. Scorching red rays flashed across the open space and struck the energy dome. The protective field, before invisible to the eye, now turned a pale pink-orange color as the heat of the rays was dissipated over the whole of the surface. In an instant the glow faded. Namon and the others were unharmed, for the moment.

At the same instant the heat rays flashed toward them, Jason leveled his force gun and fired a single pellet. In just over a second it struck the ground almost directly under the Epos leader, and even though it had been charged at minimum power, the resultant blast was still sufficient to lift the steed from the ground and throw it back several meters. It landed with a dull crash of armor, tumbling over backward, its terrified mind slaves leaping free to avoid being crushed beneath its weight.

Even as the steed struggled to right itself, the other members of the patrol were skittering back and away, seeking what cover they could find and opening fire on the formation of earthmen. Their arrogant poise had evaporated totally, and with a frenzy of firing they sought only to destroy their enemy.

Jason ordered his men to return that fire. It was a matter of survival now. Their protective energy field could absorb only so much of the blistering heat before it would collapse and leave them open to fiery death. Force pellets whistled out toward the Epos' positions, aimed not at the ground this time, but at the steeds themselves.

But the Epos had other ideas. Taking advantage of the pellets' comparatively slow velocity, the monkey marksmen took aim and with faster than human reflexes detonated the pellets before they had covered two thirds the distance. They resumed firing on the wall of energy that protected Jason and his men.

First Officer Clark frowned, sweat beading on his forehead and running down his face. "I think this is what our ancestors used to call a Mexican standoff."

"It won't be for long," Jason replied, looking at the dome of energy. His own features were bathed in sweat; the air was becoming stiflingly hot. "The power field can't take much more."

The energy dome now glowed a brilliant crimson, growing steadily weaker under the constant bombardment of the Epos' heat rays. It clearly could not last more than a few more minutes.

Jason pulled the captured heat ray pistol from his belt and thought about using it. But the Epos' armor offered them a fair amount of protection against that. Besides, he was afraid that its heat would only add to the burden of the already weakening protective field. And if that collapsed while even one of the enemy was still firing. . . .

It was tempting, though—to fight fire with fire.

Fire . . . ?

There was another possibility. It was just as risky, but it might offer a slim chance at least.

Jason quickly turned to the soldier in the center of their rough circle, the one armed with the force cannon. "Set your weapon for maximum charge," he ordered, then pointed to a spot on their right where, not far in front of the enemy position, one of the lesser treelike plants reached up to a height of fifty or sixty meters. "Fire at the base of that tree, just a bit left of center."

"Yes, sir." The man braced the force cannon on his shoulder, peered through the sight and adjusted the controls. As he triggered the firing circuit, a low hum built up in the energizing coils at the tube's front end, and a force globe whistled out.

At the same moment, Jason unleashed a sweeping salvo of pellets at the Epos. As these posed a far more immediate danger to them than the force globe, which seemed aimed not at them, the steeds concentrated their mind slaves' efforts upon the pellets. Which was exactly as Jason had hoped.

The force globe impacted with a resounding *whump!* that shook the ground beneath their feet. The erupting power of the globe splintered the base of the tree into pulp, kicking it back away and toppling the tall plant forward. With a rustle and snapping of nearby leaves and branches, the tree crashed down, slamming into the ground almost directly in front of the Epos.

The instant it came to rest, Jason leveled his captured heat ray pistol at the great trunk and fired continuously, playing the blistering beam along the whole of the plant. Within seconds, steam rose from the trunk, followed immediately by dense smoke as fire burst out and spread along its length. In a few more seconds the flames were leaping high into the air, forming an impassable barrier.

Already the Epos were falling back, instinctively recoiling from the flames as waves of heat swept over them. They could not even *see* the earthmen through that blazing curtain before them.

Jason felt sure the fire would not last more than ten minutes at most. The tissue of the tree was being consumed quickly, and with the surrounding forest area still moist from frequent rains there was not much chance of the fire spreading.

"Come on," Jason said, switching off his field unit.

The men broke their pattern and ran toward the travel tube, glad to escape, but knowing that a larger battle still awaited them. . . .

CHAPTER 14

THE CITADEL!

The small circle of people sat in a tiny chamber at the end of the travel tube, bathed in the afternoon light which filtered through the plant tissue. No one spoke. No one moved. Their breathing seemed in tune with the gentle swaying of the vine's inner fibers. Hands linked, heads bowed and eyes tightly closed, the seven people scarcely seemed alive.

They were in an extension of the vine system that reached a short way out from the hustle and bustle of the village. Laneena and Roanne were among the seven, as well as other villagers able to perceive the telepathic messages of the Epos. Individually, the distance was too great for them to catch the thought patterns in the city beyond the forest and open plain. But together, their minds linked as one, they had far greater range.

Jason watched the strange ceremony from a short distance back in the travel tube, with Namon at his side. The rest of Jason's men were back in the village, checking the equipment brought back from the *Eclipse*. Everything would have to be in perfect working order when they made their rescue attempt.

Keeping his voice low to avoid disturbing the others, Jason said, "I hope this works."

"It will." Namon's hushed tone was full of confidence. "I've seen this done before. If anything's known in the city about your people, then we'll know also."

Jason studied Roanne as he waited in the silence of the travel tube. Although in his own mind she was outshone by Laneena, Roanne was still in every way a lovely and capable young woman, and it was easy to understand Namon's interest in her. Glancing back at him, Jason said, "Laneena told me of the situation you're in . . . you and her, and Roanne."

"I'm not surprised she told you. I've seen the way she looks at you. Tell me—do you care for her?"

Jason weighed the answer in his mind a moment before finally admitting the truth. "Yes. Very much. I guess I haven't helped matters any."

"Such a simple problem," Namon said, shaking his head. "And such a difficult one. But there are more important things to consider at the moment. What do you plan to do once we know where your friends are being held?"

"A direct assault is out of the question," Jason said. "The Epos will be looking for it, and we wouldn't stand a chance. So we'll have to try something unexpected."

At that moment, there was a sound from the group of seven. A kind of collective sigh that carried with it the feeling of fear, and of dreadful awareness.

The people were coming out of their self-induced trance. Slowly, they raised their heads and blinked open eyes that had been sealed shut in concentration. Then Laneena left the others and hurried to where Jason and Namon stood.

"We know," she said.

"Where?" Jason asked, but from her look he feared he already knew the answer.

"The Citadel." She was trembling slightly, her eyes wide with knowledge of a distant horror. "The Epos are taking no chances. The patrol that captured your friends was ordered by their Most High to take them directly to the Citadel. They know from your ship and weapons that you and the others are a threat to them. To learn what they want to know, the Epos will do terrible things to your friends."

"We've got to get started at once, then," Jason said, hurrying them on. *"Let's go—"*

Darkness. . . .

That was all he could perceive at first—an impenetrable darkness that went beyond the mere absence of light. This was a darkness of the *mind* as much as of the eye.

Then gradually, Brant became aware of other sensations. A feeling of cold, and then of his own weight, resting heavily upon a hard stone surface. And then a fiery tingling, far worse than the numbness it replaced, that spread throughout his entire body and left each nerve raw and grating.

A sound came. It came again, distant and vaguely irritating, and it took Brant's jumbled auditory sense several more moments to sort it out, his mind another moment to clarify it to the point of understanding. It was not merely a sound. It was a voice—

"*Sir?*"

Brant's eyes fluttered open and he tensed, knowing he was not aboard the *Eclipse*—or anywhere *else* he ever remembered seeing for that matter. By the dim light admitted through air vents near the top of the far wall, he could make out the stone of the surrounding walls, a heavy wooden door closing off whatever lay beyond, and a group of shadowy figures standing or sitting nearby.

"Sir?" said the voice again, and this time Brant realized how close it was. He looked around and saw the lieutenant he had last seen on the cargo deck of their great ship. The man was kneeling by his side, bending over him with a look of concern.

"Thank God you're alive, sir," the man said then. "The med tech was afraid the damage from the shock was irreversible."

"Shock?" Brant said, then tried to sit up. His whole body seemed alive with tremors, muscles twitching of their own volition. Then as he steadied himself this seemed to subside. "What do you mean, shock? I was shot with something. A nerve gun, probably."

"A nerve gun?" The lieutenant sounded baffled. "But, Mr. Farand said—"

"Don't believe anything Farand said. He's the one who shot me!"

"I'm sorry, sir. I didn't know."

"Where is he? For that matter, where are *we?*"

"I think he's in the cell next to us," said the lieutenant. "With Representative Rondell. And we're all in some kind of a fortress in the mountains. The aliens brought us here this morning."

"Aliens?" Brant raised again to a sitting position, this time successfully. His eyes took in more details of the dungeonlike cell which held them. "I guess I don't have to ask if they're friendly."

"Hardly, sir. They're not even humanoid, although there *are* humans on this world. I've seen some of them here, working as slaves, or chained as prisoners."

"What about the commander and the others?"

The lieutenant shook his head. "If they're here, I haven't seen them."

Something dark and squat scuttled past them, brushing against Brant's leg as it moved. It had come from the shadows to their left and now darted toward a crevice in the rear wall.

Brant instinctively recoiled from the contact, and with the lieutenant's help got to his feet. "Don't tell me they even have *rats* here."

"Nothing so nice," the young officer told him. "They've been coming in periodically, checking us out. I think they're only scavengers, but I'm not sure."

In the slightly greater illumination at the rear wall, Brant could make out more details of the small creature. The lieutenant was right: it was no rat. It was about the right size, but the tailless thing had bristling fur that shone iridescent green. It turned to glare malevolently at them as it reached the crevice. Its primary eyes were round and glimmering, and flanked by tiny secondary eyes. A hiss of warning, or perhaps impatience, escaped through needlelike teeth that stretched in a hideously perfect row across the thing's wide face.

"I'm sorry we had to leave you on the floor," the lieutenant said. "But there's just nothing in here in the way of furniture."

"That's the least of our worries," Brant told him. "I just wish I knew whether the commander's been captured. If not, they might—"

His words halted abruptly as a scream cut through the air outside their cell. It was an all too human sound, and it came from somewhere near within the stone fortress.

The lieutenant said grimly, "They've started again."

Brant felt a sudden chill of horror, provoked by the young officer's words as much as by the scream itself. "Started *what* again? *Who?*"

"The aliens. I think they've been torturing some of their human prisoners. We've been hearing them for the last three or four hours. Maybe longer—I don't know." There was a touch of fear in the young officer's voice now, and of dread inevitability. "They haven't come for any of our men yet," he told Brant. "But I've a feeling it won't be long. . . ."

Jason stared up into the sky beyond the edge of the clearing. The late-afternoon light was quickly fading, and in less than an hour darkness would fall. He knew the timing was critical. The success of their plan hinged on it, and very likely their lives.

Through with his sightings and calculations, Jason now looked over at the giant insect carcass in the clearing. The empty shell of the grasshopperlike creature still rested where they had seen it before. The vulture bugs were gone now, having picked the inside clean. Nothing remained except the hard chitin exoskeleton, and there were changes in this now. A man-sized opening had been cut in the side of the shell with an interrupter beam, and smaller openings which would serve as view ports had been cut at intervals along the length.

Working about it were his men, except for the one soldier wounded in the fight earlier, and seven of the young village men, Namon among them. Clark left the group and approached Jason.

"The job's done, Commander," Clark said as he reached him. "A nasty bit of work, but it should do the trick."

"Good." Jason glanced toward the far side of the clearing. "What about the live ones?"

"Still grazing. I don't think the bloody things ever stop eating!"

"Do you think we can stampede them at the right time?"

"We'll launch a force globe over them. An explosion behind them should get them in the air." Clark glanced back at the hollow shell. "I just hope they'll follow us."

"They should if we're in the air first," Jason told him. "Come on, let's check out our flight system."

Clark walked with him back to the shell, where Lieutenant Cosgrove and several of the soldiers were still busily working. They had just completed securing the broad belts of the cargo lifters around the girth of the giant insect shell. Placed at regular intervals, the four belts would be capable, when operating together, of lifting the huge exoskeleton high into the air. That, and the weight of the men who would dare to fly within it.

Cosgrove was making the last cable connections, and despite the coolness of the air was sweating as if Dromii's full heat were bearing down on him. Mopping at his brow with his uniform sleeve, the boyish officer turned as he became aware of Jason's presence.

"It's all ready now, Commander," he said. "I've patched all the cables into one control unit, and rigged a second unit so you can switch over to it in case of a malfunction."

"Excellent," said Jason. "What would I do without you, T.R.?"

Cosgrove gave a worried grin. "Well, sir, let's hope you don't have to find out."

Two of the crewmen moved past them, carrying the packs of extra weapons and gear for the others once they were rescued—*if* they were rescued—while the remaining men busied themselves with last-minute checks of their equipment. Jason took leave of them and walked over to where Laneena stood apart from the group, using her mind to search for Epos patrols in the area.

"Hear anything?" Jason asked her.

"No," she said. "None of them are in the area. Are you ready to leave?"

"Yes." Jason automatically reached out to adjust the webbing harness Laneena now wore over her forest clothes, securing one of the

fasteners. "I wish you'd reconsider. This is going to be more dangerous than anything we've done yet. In the village, you'd—"

"In the village I'd have nothing to do but worry," she cut him off.
"Father didn't choose to humiliate me by ordering me to stay
behind. I don't think you will either. Besides, you'll need someone
who can read the Epos' thoughts."

He studied her another long moment, afraid for her, proud of her,
wanting her to be safe and wanting her by his side, all at the same
time. He cared for her more than he had ever thought possible, and
in spite of that—and because of it—he could not make her stay. As
if sensing the conflict of his thoughts, she smiled suddenly, en-
couragingly, disarmingly. And Jason wondered how he had ever
managed to exist during the years before he met her.

"All right," he said. "Let's go."

One by one they filed into the hollow insect shell through the
large hole cut in the side. Their positions were not critical, since the
cargo lifters would automatically compensate for any minor weight
imbalance.

First Officer Clark took a place alongside Jason. "I've served
aboard a lot of craft in my time," he said, shaking his head ruefully,
"but never a blooming bug!"

"As long as it gets us into the Citadel, that's all that matters."
Jason powered on the control unit. "Are you ready with the force
cannon?"

"Waiting for the word, Commander." Clark sighted through the
scope of the shoulder-held weapon, which now poked out through
one of the shell's small side ports. His target was a relatively clear
spot of ground just behind the herd of grazing insects.

Laneena stood directly behind Jason, hunched over like the rest
of them in the cramped space, braced for the first flight of her life.
Her features were oddly calm and unworried, despite the bizarre
situation and impending danger. Namon and the other young village
men stood poised and ready, anxiety and excitement mingling on
their faces.

"Here we go," Jason said softly. Then, with a slow, deliberate motion, he advanced the power control. The broad lift belts came
silently to life, and the great hollow exoskeleton shifted slightly as
the belts stabilized it in a level position. Jason advanced the control
a few degrees more and the shell quietly rose to a height of several
meters.

"*Seems* to be holding steady, sir," Clark observed.

"Steady enough," Jason said. "We haven't time for a real test flight." He glanced back at the others briefly, then peered out the side port at the field of grazing insects. To Clark he said, "Now's as good a time as any."

His first officer took in a deep breath and let it out, sighting carefully through the binocular scanner. He had to be sure to hit a spot close enough to the giant insects to stampede them into flight, but not so close as to injure them or send them in all directions. Slowly, his finger depressed the activator.

Power circuits closed in the big weapon. An energy globe left the chamber, passed through the arming field and whistled through the air, becoming a pale dot in the dimming light.

For brief seconds, silence. Then contact! Touching ground, the force globe released its tremendous store of energy in a blast that rocked the floor of the forest.

Instantly there came a great flurry of golden wings, a dry and raspy buzzing whose sound reached even across the distance to them. The enormous insects were leaving ground and beginning to spiral into the sky.

Jason shoved the power control forward, at the same time energizing the forward thrust circuits of the cargo lifters. The shell shot upward at a dizzying speed, beginning a course toward the mountains that lay beyond the plain and the city of the Epos.

"Are they following?" Jason demanded to know, eyes fixed ahead as he worked the controls.

"Not yet." Clark craned his head out a side opening, looking back as air rushed past him and whistled in his ears. "They're still flying in circles," he shouted over the noise, "gaining altitude, maybe. But they're not— Wait a bit, they're moving out now. They seem to be all together, and . . . yes, Commander, they are following us."

"Our luck's still holding," Jason said. "Great shot, Danny. Now if they'll stay with us, we'll have cover during our flight to the mountains. I doubt the Epos will notice one 'insect' among many."

Nearly an hour passed before they reached the mountains, having crossed the edge of the forest land and the wide, barren plain, a good kilometer north of the ancient city. Dromii had sunk beyond the horizon, the twilight had faded, and only with the reflected light of Cerus Minor were details of the landscape discernible.

"Are you sure of the position?" Jason asked Laneena.

"Yes," she answered. "Often at night, when we venture near the edge of the great plain, we have seen the strange light of the Epos, glowing on the mountain face. The sighting I gave you is right. We should be close now."

Clark stared down at the broken and irregular surface below. "There can't be many places down there level enough to build anything."

"I know." Jason made a slight readjustment of the controls. "Most of the terrain is too steep. About the only area that might be flat enough is beyond that crest over there."

Nearly a half kilometer above the lower peaks, the hollow shell flew on, reached the high and ragged ridge of stone, and passed over it. Below, several flat areas nestled among the rocks and cliffs.

"There!" Laneena cried out. "There—to the right."

Little more than a kilometer ahead of them, a strange glow could now be seen. It was situated at the end of a narrow strip of level ground, three sides of which faced steep inclines. The fourth side opened onto a sheer cliff that dropped for a distance of three hundred meters to a base of jagged, tumbled rocks.

Closer now, a structure could be made out. A massive stone fortification was the source of the light, built in a style markedly different from the ancient city in the plain. The single glow broke into a pattern of windows and courtyards where the odd, pale-blue light emerged.

Jason moved the power control back, slowly dropping the shell lower and lower. With muscles tensed and the blood suddenly pumping faster through their veins, the fourteen humans drifted closer to the forbidding structure known as the Citadel. . . .

CHAPTER 15

STRANGE ALLY

"Be ready—"

Jason said it softly, but no one missed his words. All were tensed and alert as the odd craft lost altitude, skimming the rocks and gullies. Adrenaline was bringing their senses to heightened awareness.

Clark scanned the terrain below as Jason maneuvered the shell. He suddenly pointed to a narrow line, barely visible, which ran from the level area through the high rocks. The line twisted and turned, following the pattern of ridges.

"Looks like a trail down there," Clark said. "Appears to reach down to the plain."

"Remember its location," Jason told him. "We'll have to use it later."

The shell now was only a hundred meters above the great, looming structure. As Jason dropped lower, he looked for a place to land on the roof of the building. One spot seemed better than the others —a flat area near an open courtyard at the center of the structure. Hulking objects at the corners of the roof appeared to be weapons emplacements, but they were covered and unattended. Jason steered the craft toward the landing site he had chosen.

Gently, silently, the shell touched down. Jason pulled back on the power controls, switching them off.

Moving swiftly and quietly, they disembarked from their make-shift craft and assembled on the roof. Overhead, the giant insects that had flown with them now circled, confused by the inhospitable landing site their "leader" had chosen. Then in another few moments they angled away, heading for another area of lush forest growth where food was in abundance.

Stealthily, Jason and the others moved to the edge of the roof. In the courtyard below, they could see no sign of movement. Still, there had to be guards present in the building, perhaps even patrolling on a regular basis.

Namon and several of his men uncoiled lengths of strong rope and made the ends secure to jutting projections, then let the ropes down to the courtyard. It took only a few minutes for all to climb down. So far, they had escaped discovery by the Epos, but Jason knew this could not last for long.

"Laneena," he said, "listen in on their thoughts. Probe around, see if you can get an idea of where my men are being held."

Without reply, the girl began to concentrate. Her mind cleared and became receptive to the patterns of the Epos' thoughts.

"There are many voices," she said softly after a moment. "I can't be sure, but I think the prisoners are held in cells in this direction." She gestured toward one wall of the courtyard.

There were two entrances in this wall. Which of them offered the best route into the Citadel could only be guessed. Laneena's ability could not penetrate the inner thoughts of the Epos and tap their store of knowledge. She could only receive those thoughts which were sent to others as orders or messages.

Jason chose the entrance nearest them. There would surely be connecting passageways that would allow them to detour left or right, once inside. The main problem would be the Epos themselves. Leaving the shadows, they started for the doorway.

"Energize field circuits," Jason ordered. "We'll maintain a column pattern as we move in."

In an instant, the energy field was activated and flowing around them. With the invisible wall of protective force forming an oblong shield over them, the column started through the entrance.

The interior hallway was empty. Jason noticed that although the great chunks of stone used to build the Citadel were the same as the material in the city on the great plain below, the scale of this building was different. It was smaller, and more in keeping with the equine nature of the Epos. Instead of stairs, gently sloping ramps could be seen leading to areas below. Jason tried to picture the Epos hauling rock from the city up along the trail to this place, then dismissed the thought. More likely, they had forced their human slaves to do the work. He wondered how many had died in the torturous process.

They moved deeper within the complex. The faintly bluish light of phosphorescent globes illuminated the corridor, creating an eerie atmosphere. The hallway stretched a considerable distance ahead, and the odd pattern of lights made it difficult to tell where side corridors cut through the walls. The first they encountered was not visible until they were almost upon it.

Jason had wondered about the absence of doors along the main corridor. Looking down the intersecting passageway, he saw that the entrances to rooms were located only along the one axis, north and south. They continued on past the intersection, the presence of the energy field requiring them to move down the center of the corridor.

Suddenly a sound came from just ahead. An Epos guard appeared around the corner of a narrow passageway to their left.

The horse tensed, clearly startled, then set its features in a look of fiery outrage. Its telepathic command came instantly, the tiny monkey clinging to its back rearing up, aiming a ray pistol at them and firing.

The beam of raw heat flashed out bright red in the azure gloom. It stopped abruptly barely a meter in front of Jason, splashing its energy over the invisible field surrounding them.

Jason's force gun was already drawn, set at minimum power. He fired barely a second after the heat ray struck their energy field. In an instant the pellet struck the guard, sending it stumbling back into the passageway.

But too late to prevent the alarm—

A telepathic alert had been sounded. The sound of rapid hoofbeats came from several directions, and more guards were coming down the passageway to their right. There was no more time for stealth. The battle was on!

"*Danny,*" Jason snapped. "Reset for maximum power. Aim for the roof; we've got to close that corridor."

Clark was readjusting his weapon even as he aimed. He fired. His force pellet whizzed out, almost in tandem with Jason's shot.

With a rumbling crash, a whole section of the roof collapsed, piling stone and timbers high in the passageway, completely blocking it. The approaching guards found themselves faced with an insurmountable obstacle.

Running quickly now, Jason and the others continued along the corridor, blocking the side passages as they went. A fine mist of stone dust hung in the air, assailing their nostrils and clouding their view, and swirling with their swift passage.

At the end of the hallway, side corridors led off in both directions. For a moment, the group of fourteen halted.

To Laneena, Jason said, "Which way?"

She frowned, concentrating, trying to pull some idea of the location out of the riot of thoughts that now surged through the Citadel. "This way, to the left, I think."

They had not gone more than a meter down the new corridor when a barrage of shots fired at them from behind struck their energy field. More guards were approaching from that direction.

"*Namon*—" Jason shouted, but did not have to finish it.

Behind him, Namon and his men from the village had set up a barrage of their own. The volley brought the roof down, closing that corridor behind them as well.

Whole sections of the Citadel were now closed off from the rest of the rooms and corridors. Jason hoped that as many guards as possible were on the other side of the blocked areas. Whatever the case, he and the others could only go forward now, toward whatever lay ahead.

Abruptly they reached the termination of the corridor. An opening to the right led into a large room, perhaps five by ten meters in size. Plunging into the chamber, they immediately caught the ray fire of a guard at the other end. A volley of force pellets whizzed back with stunning impact, sending the guard toppling to the flooring.

The threat ended, they looked about the room. Four massive wooden doors were located along one wall.

Jason approached the first, drew close to the heavy panel and listened carefully. His hand touched it and felt little resistance. He shoved it open, his weapon trained inside. The door banged against the interior wall with a creaking moan, sending a dozen or more rat-sized creatures scurrying for holes and crevices in the stone.

Laneena stifled a scream, averting her eyes. Several of the men gasped at the sight before them.

Inside the cell, a hideous form was shackled to the wall. The awful thing that dangled limply from its chains was little more than a skeleton, its bones barely held together by shredded flesh. A human being once, but alive no more. Jason reached in and pulled the door shut, his face grim.

He found the second door locked. Listening closely, he thought he heard a sound on the other side. It might have been a whisper of a voice, or merely the dry rustle of tiny claws upon stone. He decided to call out.

"Brant?"

At first there was only a cautious silence. Then . . .

"Commander . . . is that you?" The tone was relieved and incredulous.

Jason pulled his interrupter from his webbing, setting the beam for narrow spread and limited depth. "Is everyone all right?"

"So far," Brant's voice shot back. "Some of the others are in another cell. I'm not sure how many."

"Hang on," Jason answered. He aimed the interrupter at the lock and fired. There was a hiss of sound as the beam ionized air in the line of fire, then the lock fell neatly in two, dropping to the floor. Without moving from the spot where he stood, he fired a beam at the locks on the remaining two doors. He pushed the door nearest him open. Brant and approximately half the crew that had remained behind at the *Eclipse* stared out at him, joy flooding faces etched with fatigue and fear.

Then a startling attack!

Jason suddenly felt the searing impact of a heat ray. In leaving the protective radius of the group energy field, he had exposed himself to fire. The weaker field of his individual unit was not enough to protect him completely.

Surprised he was still alive and standing, he wheeled about and fired his interrupter at the pistol aimed in his direction. The beam disabled the weapon instantly. Then Jason stared in disbelief at the guard who had fired at him.

For the guard was *human*. Four of them, three young men and a girl, had entered through a doorway at the end of the room.

Dressed in plain garments, each wore the same kind of communicator medallion Old Stod had worn in the city below. Armed with knives, only the foremost man of the group had been entrusted with a ray pistol by his masters. He now discarded the useless weapon and leaped forward, drawing his curved blade from its sheath.

For a brief moment, Jason and the others hesitated. He was caught off guard, surprised by the fact that humans would willingly be guards for the Epos and attack their own kind.

In the second he waited before firing, the interrupter was knocked from his hand. Swiftly upon him, the guard sought to bring his blade down in an arcing slash. Jason instinctively grabbed the man's wrists, holding them locked in a deadly test of strength.

Clark aimed his force gun, but could not use it. Jason was in his line of fire, and too close to the others in the struggle to risk a shot.

"He needs help," Clark snapped. "We'll have to drop the energy field—"

Jason heard him. *"No*—maintain your field. There may be other armed guards in the area."

But the imprisoned men in the second cell had no energy field to risk losing. Brant and several of the others charged out. Their strength had been sapped by the long trek up the mountain, but they plunged into the battle with all they could muster.

The two remaining guardsmen held off the prisoners at a short distance with savage knife thrusts, but Brant and his men were working around on all sides. The guards could eventually be overcome by sheer numbers.

Seeing an opening in the crowd, the girl left the side of her two fellow guards and worked her way toward Jason. His back was toward her now and she turned her curved blade downward, raising it high in both hands.

"*No!*" Laneena cried out. She had seen the girl coming and was already running toward her. Once free of the energy field's range, she switched off her own device.

She slammed headlong into the girl, knocking the knife from her hands. Tumbling to the floor, they twisted and turned, trying to break each other's hold. Still fighting, they rolled toward the wall, barely missing injury in the battle around them.

Then matters became worse.

Four more guardsmen entered from the end of the room. Traitorous humans like the rest, these were all armed with ray pistols. But an odd weapons standoff had developed. They could not fire without the risk of hitting their fellow guards. Clark and the others could not fire for fear of hitting their own people.

The four new guardsmen began to advance toward the melee, seemingly with the intention of subduing their enemies at close range. Clark prepared to disregard Jason's order to maintain their energy field.

Neither he nor the guards had noticed the door to the fourth cell swinging open. It had moved slowly, haltingly, as if with some effort. Now it was open, and the way out clear. But what emerged from the cell was not a human.

Five hundred and fifty kilograms of fighting terror sprang into the room. Jet-black hide glistening, the horse that now dove into the battle was the same in appearance as the other Epos, except that no monkey served as its mind slave. But it was apparent that its enemies were the same as Jason's.

Kicking savagely, he scattered the new guardsmen before they knew what hit them. Brant and the others hastened to retrieve the fallen weapons, as did the guards armed only with knives. In the scramble that followed, the horse dove in again, snapping at the traitorous humans, and succeeding in kicking one into the now vacated cell.

The strange new twist to the fight had startled Jason, but it had startled more the man he battled. His guard down, he failed to react in time as Jason released his hold and brought a fist up under the man's chin with all his force. The guard staggered back, falling to the floor, where he slumped motionless.

In the confusion of fighting men and flailing hooves, no one seemed to notice the girl wrest an arm free and strike Laneena. Breaking free of her hold, the girl backed off a step, spied a fallen knife on the floor and seized it. Hatred blazing in her eyes, she lunged at Laneena. . . .

CHAPTER 16

THE GENERALS

Laneena's fiery red hair hung in disordered curls. Weakened by her struggle, she leaned against the wall, trying to catch her breath. A sound alerted her. She looked up and saw the female guard's violent lunge, saw her eyes and the flashing blade. There was no time to react, to fight back, to do anything.

Then abruptly, Laneena felt herself being jerked sideways, out of the path of death. The guard missed her target by a hairsbreadth, colliding with the wall headfirst. Stunned, she slid to the floor and did not stir.

Jason released his hold on Laneena's arm and steadied her. If he had not turned in time to see what was happening, if he had been too slow in moving . . . He shoved the thought from his mind.

For now, the battle was over.

Not a single guard remained standing. Brant gathered up the fallen weapons while one of the other men checked the end doorway through which the guards had entered the room. Clark directed his group to drop their energy field and sent Namon to watch the front corridor entrance. With both ends of the room guarded, there would be little chance of another surprise attack.

"You'll be needing a new medpac, Commander."

Jason turned his head as his first officer pulled a case from the rear of his webbing harness and showed it to him. The fabric covering was almost totally incinerated, and the polyceramic shell of the medpac was scorched on its outer surface. A quick glance within showed that its contents were reduced to a molten sludge, the medical preparations and dressings now useless.

"Lucky that ray shot hit this," Clark said. "It would have gone through most anything else."

Jason smiled thinly. "Maybe there's something to preventive medicine after all."

He turned his attention now to the horse-creature that stood nearby. The equine warrior studied the men with cautious eyes, but did not seem hostile.

"Laneena," Jason asked, "can you communicate with him?"

She looked toward the horse, but did not have a chance to speak.

"It is not necessary." The words had not been spoken. Yet they had been heard, in the minds of Jason and the others.

Jason addressed him. "Who are you? Why did you help us?"

The creature paused a moment before replying. "I am Tano, a high soldier—what you would call an officer. I fought the guards to help myself as much as to help you."

"But why? You're an Epos."

"And you are a human, as are the guards we fought." The steed paused. "The Epos here in this fortress and the city beyond are outcasts—criminals."

Jason puzzled over Tano's silent words. He turned slightly as he saw the door of the third cell opening. Oleg Rondell emerged, cautiously surveying the scene before him to be certain the fighting was over. He was followed by Zelig Farand and the remainder of the captured crew. The injured still bore the scars of the crash. Those with broken limbs moved a bit more slowly than the rest, although the breaks had been fused by rapid-heal techniques in the *Eclipse*'s medical unit. The temporary light alloy braces would soon be unnecessary.

Returning his attention to Tano, Jason asked, "How do you know our language? Do you read our thoughts?"

"No," he replied. "But I hear your voices, as I hear all sounds. I come from a settlement far to the north, called Trenos. Long ago, a colony of humans settled nearby."

"The Northlanders?" Laneena asked with sudden interest.

"As you call them. We learned that we could not receive their thoughts, since all but a few humans lack the necessary control of their minds. Your race developed speech for communication. Ours developed telepathy. But by studying your spoken language we developed a mental technique which could be used to project our thoughts on a level humans can perceive. It requires some effort."

"Odd," Jason said, still dubious. "The Epos here seem unaware of the technique."

"None but a few have bothered to study your language, and then only those words which are of use to them in controlling slaves. The evil ones here think humans are fit only for menial work."

First Officer Clark addressed the steed. "You've not yet told us why you were imprisoned, or what brought you here."

"The answer to both is the same: because I was sent here to spy on them." Tano tossed his head impatiently. "The rest you shall learn later, but now I must reach their laboratory. The equipment they took from me is stored there. Without it, I cannot contact my settlement and warn them, or request aid. And without help, none of us can hope to win. By now, the alert will have been sounded in the city below. Reinforcements will be coming up the mountain to attack us."

Oleg Rondell barged forward. "Smith—do you seriously intend to take this creature at its word? How can we trust him?"

Jason ignored him. "Danny—take half the men in your group, Namon and T.R. will take the rest. You'll have more flexibility that way. Hand out the spare equipment we brought from the ship."

Clark nodded. "Then what?"

"Find an outer wall. Wait there, use your energy fields for protection and activate your tracer signal so I'll be able to find you quickly."

"Where will you be?"

"I'm going with Tano to find that laboratory. If what he says is true, we have as much to gain as he does in sending a message to his friends. The shell we flew here in won't hold us all, and although there's still a chance we can fight our way down that trail, we'd be a lot better off with help."

Laneena had dusted herself off and straightened her gear. Rather than join the groups, she moved quickly to Jason's side. "I'm going with you," she said.

Jason offered no argument. There seemed to be as much risk one way as the other. Taking one of the captured ray pistols Brant had collected, he handed it to her.

"Here," he told her. "You may need this."

"Quickly," Tano urged telepathically. "We must hurry!"

Everyone headed for the doorway at the end of the room. On the other side they found themselves in a chamber twice as large. Crude wooden tables bore straps for binding prisoners, and their surfaces were stained from previous tortures and unspeakable surgical experiments. Testing equipment, scalpels and other instruments were arranged upon shelves along the walls.

And two doorways. To the left, a corridor led away to other areas. To the right, a ramp sloped down into a lower level of the Citadel.

Tano moved toward the ramp. "Their laboratory is this way—near the center of the building."

"Take the corridor, Danny," Jason ordered. "We'll meet you as soon as possible."

"Good luck, Commander," Clark said, then hurried the others off.

The glistening steed trotted down the ramp, with Jason and Laneena keeping as close behind him as possible. Checking his force gun, Jason found it almost empty of pellets. He quickly snapped a fresh pod into place.

"Tano," he asked as they ran, "can help arrive from Trenos in time?"

"Perhaps," came the mental reply. "We have means of transportation not given to the outcasts. They were banished without equipment . . . without even the rare elements needed to produce it. They were allowed to keep only minor weapons needed for their self-defense."

Minor weapons, Jason thought. If the high-powered heat ray pistols and paralysis guns he had seen were considered minor weapons, then what did Tano's friends possess?

The ramp plunged deep into the Citadel's interior, then leveled off into a corridor. At the end of the corridor stood a great wooden door, two meters wide and three meters high.

Tano slowed his pace. "The quarters of the outcast leaders lie ahead; beyond that is the laboratory. Have your weapons ready."

They approached the door. Weapons drawn, Jason and Laneena waited. Turning abruptly, Tano tilted forward on his front legs and kicked mightily at the door.

Splintering fragments fell as the heavy panel was torn from its hinges. It seemed to shudder in the air for a moment, then fell to the stone floor with a resounding thud.

Jason sprayed a burst of force pellets in a sweeping pattern. It was intended more to surprise than to injure—to gain the firepower advantage—and it did exactly that.

Four Epos guards scattered out of the way of the exploding force pellets. One of them was knocked from his feet by the concussion wave of a near-miss.

Then in the next instant, Laneena fired wildly with her ray pistol, setting up such an unpredictable pattern of scorching beams that no guard dared stop his headlong flight long enough to aim his own weapon. She stopped abruptly when Tano leaped past her into the chamber.

The ebony steed charged into the path of two guards, hooves driving out like twin battering rams. But these guards would not be easily defeated. They were the honored protectors of their rulers, and would fight with their last ounce of strength.

Jason dove suddenly to the floor, a searing ray blast scorching the air where he had stood just seconds before. Rolling to one side as a second ray hit the floor near him, he fired a volley of pellets. His aim was close enough and two of the guards were toppled. But now a new danger came.

"Jason, look out!"

At Laneena's warning, he saw the two remaining guards in close battle with Tano. They were almost upon him, and he might at any second be trampled.

Timing his moves carefully, he scuttled past the hooves of the horse nearest him. Dodging and twisting, he worked his way out of the range of their struggle. There was no way to fire his force gun at the guards without risking injury to Tano.

Laneena seemed to sense the reason behind his hesitancy. She took careful aim with the heat ray. It failed to fire, its charge depleted. Discarding it, she saw the fallen weapons of the other guards and scrambled for them. Grabbing the two closest pistols, she whirled and aimed one of them, firing. But instead of a heat ray—

A stun beam caught one of the guards as it reared to strike Tano. Its muscles locked and the horse toppled sideways to the floor, where it lay still.

Tano now had but one enemy to fight. Locked in close combat, the startling battle raged on, both on a physical and a mental level. The Epos guard sought to have its mind slave fire at Tano, but the ebony steed began to concentrate his own will upon the tiny beast.

Held in the grip of two powerful minds, the monkey tensed. Its muscles fought against each other as conflicting orders battered its brain. Eyes glazing, the furry creature began to waver. Slowly, with agonizing effort, it began to turn its ray pistol toward its own master.

Panicked by the realization it had lost control over its mind slave, the Epos guard abruptly turned its head to snap at the tiny creature, and in the moment its attention was diverted Tano lashed out, quickly subduing the guard.

For a moment, the great chamber was quiet.

Jason slipped a fresh pellet pod from the string and snapped it onto the force gun. He made a quick check of the remaining pods. Only five were still fully loaded.

Ignoring his bruises and cuts, Tano advanced toward the line of decorated partitions that divided the chamber. Jason and Laneena followed as the ebony steed pushed open a section of the ornamental barrier.

This part of the chamber was larger and more ornately furnished. Tapestrylike wall hangings covered much of the bare stone, and large bowls of fruit, vegetables and grains were scattered about low tables.

Movement to their right caught Jason's attention.

Transparent screens of a thick amber-colored material were locking into place across the rear half of the chamber. On the other side of these barriers were the high rulers of the outcast settlement. Three mighty stallions, no doubt the equivalent of generals in this military society, stood poised there, facing them. Each had four or five tiny mind slaves clinging to its woven covering, each of these brandishing a weapon. Behind the stallions were their mares and young, hastily fleeing the chamber through a secret passage in the rear wall. Once they were through, the high rulers themselves turned and followed through the emergency escape route.

"More guards will come!" Tano said urgently.

"In that case," Jason replied, "we'd better find that laboratory fast. . . ."

CHAPTER 17

THE DOOMSDAY MECHANISM

A doorway at the end of the grand chamber led into a short corridor. Tano again led the way, with Jason and Laneena following at a rapid pace.

Jason wondered how long it might take guards trapped in the other side of the Citadel to clear away the rubble that blocked their way. One of the few things that had kept the humans from being outnumbered thus far was their extensive blocking of corridors and connecting halls. But how long could it last?

Suddenly, Tano slid to an abrupt halt, almost turning sideways in his haste. Forced to stop behind him, Jason and Laneena peered ahead. Only now did they see what the steed's sharp eyes had spotted.

A section of the dark stone flooring had slid aside no more than a meter ahead of them. Light from the phosphorescent globes dotting the corridor reached down into the pit, but failed to reveal a bottom. They had almost run headlong into a deadly trap.

Only a narrow strip of flooring ran along each side of the hole, barely wide enough for humans, and far too narrow for a horse. Jason started out along the ledge, sidestepping, his back to the wall. Laneena followed in like manner. Reaching the spot where the flooring was solid again, they looked back.

Tano looked across, gauging the distance. He then backed partway down the corridor and stopped. Nostrils flaring, he suddenly shot forward. At the last possible second, his mighty hind legs kicked out, propelling him across the gaping pit.

There was a moment's terrible uncertainty in which it seemed he might not make it, that his jump might fall short of the distance required, and he would plummet into the depths below. Then his front hooves came down just beyond the edge, his rear hooves almost at the very edge. Only his momentum carried him safely past the point of danger. Without even pausing for a deep breath, Tano continued forward.

At the end of the corridor they found a massive metal door in the wall to the right. Jason looked, but found no handles or controls by which to open it. He was not sure they had enough time to try cutting through it with a heat ray pistol. The metal had the look of a heat-resistant alloy.

"Is there some way to open this?" he asked.

"Yes," Tano replied. "But only by a telepath. The latch must be released by a mental command."

The horse concentrated, searching the wall with its mind for the hidden lock. Locating it, Tano directed a command at the device. Mechanisms whirred deep within the wall, and within seconds the massive metal door began to slide open. Cautiously, they entered.

The incredible laboratory seemed empty of guards. Only the faint sounds of equipment operating could be heard. High towers of pulsing lights created an eerie glow within the chamber. Tano directed the door to close. As the thick metal slab locked again into place, Jason turned to the telepathic steed.

"Is there another way in here?"

"No. This is the only door."

"Then to get at us, guards will have to come the same way we did. They can probably get across the pit . . . maybe even move the flooring back in place." Jason paused, studying the laboratory. "Tano, is there a corridor running near one of these walls?"

The steed indicated the far wall with a jerk of his head. "That one."

"Good enough." Jason pulled his interrupter from its case, having retrieved it after the battle in the cell block. Aiming toward the wall near the door, he asked, "Where is the lock mechanism?"

"On the left side, about level with your shoulders."

Jason adjusted his aim and fired. Except for the thin crisscross lines which now appeared in the stone, nothing seemed to have changed. But the circuits of the lock device had been neatly sliced through in a number of directions. The door could no longer be opened.

Laneena suddenly froze in terror. "Look!"

The others turned in time to see it . . . the dark form of some strange creature. Cloaked in dusk-gray garments, the thing was vaguely humanoid, but oddly angular, with a wide, flat torso and narrow tapering limbs. There was just a glimpse of a hideous skull-like face, framed within a dark helmet, as it darted from behind a bank of equipment. Then amazingly, it jumped sideways and disappeared into thin air. Only a faint wavering of light rays marked the spot. An instant later . . . nothing!

Jason stared in amazement, his weapon pointing at empty space. Tano seemed equally startled, offering no comment at all.

"That explanation you said would come later," Jason addressed him. "Maybe you'd better tell me now."

"I cannot explain what just happened." Tano began searching for something among equipment littering a counter.

"The rest of it then. You said the Epos here were banished without equipment . . . yet this lab! What are they doing here?"

Tano hesitated a moment before sending the answer into their minds. "They are preparing a weapon which will destroy Trenos, the settlement of which I told you." He continued looking along the next counter. "Many years ago, a group of scientists and warriors in Trenos began conducting forbidden experiments. They developed a weapon of terrible destructive power. Their goal was to use that weapon to overthrow our leaders and place themselves in control. They failed. We destroyed their equipment and banished them forever from the settlement. Years passed. Criminals and outlaws banished from our city came here and joined the others. Then recently, we found evidence of test sites destroyed by the same type of weapon. The sites are not far from here, at increasing ranges from this laboratory."

Jason thought back, remembering the strangely blighted areas of landscape he had seen when the *Eclipse* plummeted to the planet's surface. His mental image of those kilometers of festering growth brought a terrible significance to Tano's words.

"If used uncontrolled," Tano continued, "the weapon might destroy all plant and animal life here forever. We had lost one world already. We were not about to lose another."

"You're not of this planet?"

"No. We traveled here from another world, far distant. Our own was becoming uninhabitable. The atmosphere became toxic to all life, and our race left on four great colonizer ships, searching space for another planet on which we could live. The ship my ancestors piloted landed here."

Tano found what he was looking for on the counter. The device looked like some ornamental collar, with its wide silver mesh band

and jewellike fixtures. But the jewels were upon closer look solid-state circuitry of alien design. The steed picked it up gently in its teeth and turned to Jason.

"You will have to put it on for me," Tano directed. "Around my neck, the fastening toward the back."

Jason complied, putting the strange device in place.

"We use these to amplify our thoughts and send them over great distances." Tano then fell silent and seemed to concentrate.

Jason could perceive nothing of the beamed thought message, and realized that he could hear Tano's thoughts only when purposely directed at him. However, Laneena could obviously hear them even now, and was studying the content of the message. Her knowledge of the Epos' language was limited, but she seemed to find nothing alarming in the transmitted thoughts. Her expression remained calm.

"It is done," Tano told them at last, once more on a level they could perceive. "They have been warned and are sending help. But we still must destroy the weapon."

"We'll have to find it first," Jason replied.

Looking around the banks of equipment, Jason recognized some things similar to those of Earth's technology. Other things were vastly different, their purpose obscure. The tall, pulsing towers of light were drawing power from somewhere, but from what source? There was a great multitude of equipment on all sides, but nothing that seemed to be the weapon Tano had mentioned.

"It must be here!" The steed seemed frantic now. "Only in this laboratory could they build and operate such a weapon."

Jason said nothing, wondering if he had placed too much confidence in their new ally.

Laneena had been searching along the walls. Now at the end of the chamber, she paused, listening. Then suddenly she walked forward to the wall . . . and abruptly disappeared!

"*Jason—*" Her melodic voice called out from nowhere. "I think I've found it!"

Jason and Tano ran to the spot where she had last been seen. Suddenly, she appeared again, out of nowhere.

"This way," she said, excited and astonished. "The wall here—it is not real, only an illusion."

They followed her, and to their own astonishment passed through the point where the wall appeared to be. The true chamber was nearly twice the length it seemed. Looking back, they could still see the other half of the room, but through a hazy barrier of some kind that cut across the laboratory.

"Something is wrong!" Tano told them. "We have no devices capable of producing an effect like that. These outcasts could not have advanced so far beyond our own science."

"That barrier," said Jason, "isn't the only thing out of place here."

They could see he was right, for the equipment in this hidden section of the laboratory looked nothing like the rest they'd seen. At one side, powerful generators fed energy to rows of odd devices—devices that were as far removed from the Epos' regular equipment as Jason's weapons were from the villagers' primitive spears and knives.

But the most fantastic of all the devices was the bizarre thing in the center of the chamber.

A cylinder of solid crystal, three meters in length, stood upright. It seemed not to rest directly upon the floor, but floated a short distance above it. Encased within the solid crystal form was a metallic robot, bronze in color and subtly nonhuman in shape. A myriad of glowing lights surrounded it, and the entire lower section of the robot was encased in a mass of circuits and energy cells.

Tano stopped before the control console of one device that seemed more like the Epos' equipment in the other part of the chamber. "This is the weapon of which I spoke. But nothing else here is of our science."

"Then there's only one answer," Jason said uneasily. "The outcasts have been receiving help from some alien group we know nothing about. All we can be sure of is that they're incredibly advanced."

The ebony steed turned his attention to the weapon before him. Directing mental commands at the console, he energized the power circuits. An array of gas-filled tubes around a central energy globe began to glow. In the center of the console, a view screen brightened, forming an image. It was focused on a city, the heart of the settlement directly at the intersection of the screen's converging target indicators.

Tano stiffened. "Trenos . . . it is already aimed at Trenos. They have completed their work sooner than I expected."

At that moment, from behind them came a sound. The muffled tone of heat ray pistols came from the hall outside the laboratory.

"They're trying to burn through the door," Jason said quickly. "We haven't much time."

"Destroy the weapon!" Tano urged. "It must not be used."

"Stand back." Jason leveled his force gun at the still activated device, set it for maximum power, and fired. Only one pellet whizzed out of the arming tube. Only one was needed.

On contact, the pellet discharged its full store of energy. Jason had aimed at the foremost edge of the console, so that the concussion wave would not hurl any part of the debris back toward them. In less than a second, the blast had leveled the strange weapon, reducing it to useless rubble.

"What about the rest of the equipment?" Tano asked.

Jason returned his gaze to the center of the chamber. "Unless I'm wrong, that cylinder operates as some kind of control monitor over all of it."

"Hurry!" Laneena cried out. "They're almost through!"

The massive metal door of the laboratory was now glowing bright red. A sputtering dot of white light in the center marked the point where perhaps a dozen heat ray beams converged.

Jason aimed quickly at the weird alien machine floating just above the floor. He wondered if it had a protective defense screen. Jason had no idea whether, built by some unknown race, it possessed weapons of its own. But he fired upon it anyway.

The pellet struck it dead center. As the energy flare faded, the cylinder remained where it had been, and at first Jason thought the incredible device was undamaged. Then minute cracks began radiating out from the point of contact—cracks that widened and spread across the crystal.

Abruptly, energy discharges flashed within the cylinder. Circuits fused together in molten masses as the pattern of pulsing lights became erratic. It had not been destroyed, but it had been severely damaged.

Jason wished they could somehow take the device with them. Studying it might reveal much about the unknown aliens. But the thought was short-lived. The cylinder suddenly faded from view, as if drawn back to its mysterious source.

Uncontrolled, the mighty power plants began to pulse at a dangerous rate. Glowing brighter, they emitted a high-pitched whine that steadily increased in volume. Locked in a runaway reaction, they would reach detonation state in a matter of minutes.

"Let's go," Jason said. "They won't use this lab again."

They raced toward the far wall, Jason firing a volley of pellets at the stone surface. With a rumbling roar, a section of the wall slammed outward. Continuing on through the opening, the three emerged in the corridor beyond, on the opposite side of the laboratory from the true entrance. They had barely cleared the impromptu doorway when the clatter of hooves came from behind them.

The guards had made it through the door!

Tano addressed Jason and Laneena. "You can't outrun them on your own. Get on my back, quickly."

Without hesitating, Jason swung up to the steed's back. Pulling Laneena up behind him, he told her, "Use your energy field. Both of our devices may be enough to give us all some protection, at least."

Tano took off at a fast gallop as the energy field formed an invisible dome around them. Laneena clung tightly to Jason, who clutched the edge of Tano's woven covering. Head low, the steed sought to put as much distance as possible between them and the pursuing guards.

Already, rays were flashing toward them. Those that did not miss entirely were absorbed by the energy field. Although the combined field of the two units was strong enough to disperse the heat rays, it could not long withstand the sustained barrage now directed at them. Glowing fiery red, the energy field was clearly visible in a matter of seconds. And it could not absorb all of that heat. . . .

Hurrying down a wide corridor on the far side of the Citadel, First Officer Clark's group and the group led by Namon and Lieutenant Cosgrove searched for a way out of the massive complex. They ran in as tight a formation as their haste would permit, their energy shields linked and their weapons ready.

"This place is a ruddy maze," Clark said, more to himself than to the soldiers with him. "There's *got* to be an outside wall somewhere hereabouts."

"We're all as good as dead," Oleg Rondell muttered a short distance behind him. "It's all Smith's fault. *All* Smith's fault."

The words reached Clark's sharp ears and angered him. He was about to forsake his officer's code of behavior and tell Rondell exactly what he could do with his complaints, in graphic detail, when suddenly from the cross corridor ahead of them appeared a half dozen Epos guards.

Ray pistols buzzed and dazzling ruby beams hissed their way toward them, brightening the corridor's walls with their pink glow. The peculiar burned-air odor came through the energy shield, but the beams did not, instead splashing their radiance over the curve of the invisible field.

Before that glow had faded, Clark fired reflexively, a burst of pellets streaming out from his force gun. Two of the Epos received direct enough hits to be knocked from their feet, collapsing to the hard flooring, stunned and injured. The others skittered back, retreating as some of the pellets made contact with the wall at the corridor's corner and sent shattered chunks of stone flying.

"This way, lads!" Clark yelled, directing them down the cross corridor to their right, directly away from the path taken by the retreating Epos guards. It also stood the best chance of leading them to an outer wall.

The men hurried on, following Clark's lead as stone dust hung in the air about them. The second group had just rounded the corner and started down the new corridor when Lieutenant Cosgrove's attention was abruptly riveted by something a short distance back from the ruined wall.

Where the Epos guards had fallen, their tiny mind slaves were scattering, confused and terrified now that their masters' mental control was momentarily lacking. But one of the small monkeys could not flee. A large chunk of stone had pinned the end of its tail to the floor, holding it fast despite its frantic struggles. And the wall was still crumbling—

"Jeez!" Cosgrove's boyish features set in a frown of concern. Maybe he shouldn't care about the tiny creatures, he thought, but in a way the mind slaves were as much victims of the Epos as the humans were. Mindless of the danger, Cosgrove left the group and the safety of the shield, dropping back.

Something made Clark look around then, and he rapped out, "Get back here! *Lieutenant? T.R.?*"

But Cosgrove did not heed him. He reached the corner where the collapsing wall threatened the pinned creature and quickly knelt. He reached out and grasped the chunk of rock, cautious at first, fearing the frightened monkey might bite him. The stone was heavy, and there were more of similar size and lethal nature grating and shifting in the ruined wall beside him.

"T.R.!" Clark called again, sharper this time. *"Look out!"*

Cosgrove glanced up. The four remaining Epos guards had halted their retreat and two of them had turned. Cosgrove saw the flash of their pistols even as he started to duck. There wasn't even time to reactivate the energy shield he had turned off as he neared the monkey.

The first shot was completely off target and passed on down the corridor to scorch the wall beyond the intersection. The second shot was much closer, and would have struck him full in the chest had he not ducked. As it was, the edge of the beam touched his shoulder, charring the material of his uniform and searing the flesh beneath it.

Wincing with the sudden pain, eyes watering, he brought up his force gun and fired a burst of pellets blindly. They landed with a dull *whump,* bringing down more stone at the far end of the corridor, partially blocking it. Beyond the rubble and the haze of dust, he could make out the guards' renewed retreat, disappearing around a corner. He had not even touched them.

Still wincing with pain, and as angry at himself as he was with the Epos, Cosgrove seethed with expletives he could not bring himself to utter. *"You—you—"* he blustered after the retreating forms, then finally found partial satisfaction as he yelled, "may all your offspring be geldings!"

Then a deep rumble in the wall beside him brought his mind back to more pressing matters. That last burst of shots had not helped the crumbling wall in the least.

Quickly seizing the stone which pinned the monkey's tail, he wrenched it free and released the tiny mind slave. Then he stumbled back away as the wall began to collapse around him. The monkey leaped directly at him even as he moved, clutching at his webbing harness, and the two of them just got clear of the area when several monstrous chunks of stone crashed down where they had been.

Cosgrove breathed a sigh of relief, then tried to disengage the tiny creature from his webbing harness. The monkey would have no part of it. It was not about to be abandoned again amid all this commotion. So be it, Cosgrove decided. He turned and ran to rejoin the others, not about to waste any more precious time. . . .

In another corridor somewhere below them, Tano raced on with his human burdens, the pursuing guards still maintaining the pace behind him, and still firing. The temperature within the protective energy field had risen to a stifling level, making the simple act of breathing difficult.

Jason could not turn fully around with Laneena behind him, but he managed to bring his force gun around in a firing position. With a wide fanning motion, he emptied the pod of its remaining pellets.

Chunks of rock and ceiling timbers crashed into the corridor, blocking the way. No longer did the ray beams flash.

Jason faced forward again, and with a free finger of his gun hand activated his comset. The clear, bleeping tone of Clark's tracer signal began.

The corridor flooring rose as a ramp led up to a higher level.

Behind them, the high-pitched whine of the generators rose in volume, until the foundations of the Citadel seemed to throb with its vibrations. Tano ascended the ramp at top speed, reaching the upper level in less than a minute.

"Which way?" his words fairly screamed in their minds.

Jason looked down at the tiny indicator on the comset's top surface. "To the right."

An intersecting hallway cut across the corridor twenty meters ahead. Tano reached it and made a tight turn to the right.

Somewhere ahead of them, Clark and the others waited. If they could only reach the outer wall in time, and escape before the generators reached detonation stage!

From a side corridor to the left, a squad of Epos guards emerged. Jason prepared for a fight, but the Epos raced past them without more than a glance. In other parts of the Citadel now, the Epos were running. Panic swept through the great fortress as the throbbing drone of the overloading power generators grew louder, and telepathic warnings were sounded. There seemed to be only one order given . . . one order obeyed: *Evacuate!*

Tano reached the end of the corridor. But Jason was watching carefully the route ahead, and answered before the question could be asked.

"Still to the right—"

No more resistance was met as the ebony steed sped forward. The way ahead seemed deserted.

Then, rounding an angle of the hallway, they caught sight of the others. Clark had found an outer wall. Both groups were in a defensive position that showed they were still maintaining their energy fields.

Ventilation windows were along the wall at regular intervals, but too high and too narrow to use for escape. Several of the soldiers were attempting to cut through the stone with captured heat ray pistols, but were making slow progress.

Clark looked around with relief as Tano galloped up with Jason and Laneena. He quickly ordered the men to switch off their energy fields. There was little need for them now.

Jason and Laneena had already turned off their units, and as the steed halted in front of Clark they quickly dismounted. Clark stepped forward to greet his commander.

"I was about ready to come looking for you," he told him. "This place sounds as if it's ready to blow sky-high!"

"It is." Jason caught sight of the tiny monkey clinging to Cosgrove's webbing harness. "Where'd that come from?"

"Long story, Commander," Clark said. "Tell you later. Did you run across a way out of here?"

"Not where we were."

"Neither did we. And I wasn't about to ask the Epos for directions. Do you think there's a door nearby? The wall's thicker here than the inner ones. Even the force guns may not do the job."

"We'll have to try," Jason said. "There's no time to look around."

Motioning the others aside, Jason went to the wall and pulled his interrupter from its case. Setting it for full power, he held it close to the wall and triggered it, slowly swinging the device in a wide arc that ran from the floor to up over his head and back down again on the other side. A groove etched itself deeply into the stone, cutting perhaps halfway through the wall in some places. He then sliced more lines vertically through the large semicircular section.

Stripping the fully loaded pellet pod from his force gun, Jason now wedged it into a crevice between two of the stone blocks. Setting his force gun for maximum power, he held it near enough the pod for the weapon's arming field to energize the pellets.

"Get back!" he said to the others, moving them a safe distance down the corridor. Reaching the soldier who carried the powerful force cannon, he ordered the weapon from him.

"If this works," Jason told everyone, "be ready to run." He shouldered the force cannon, energized its circuits, and took aim at the pod of charged pellets wedged into the center of the scored wall. He fired.

The globe of contained energy shot out, reaching the wall in an instant. Its own massive power combined with that of the charged pellets, and the resultant jolt as it struck seemed enough to bring the Citadel down around their ears.

Cracking along the lines scored by the interrupter beam, huge sections of the stone wall shuddered outward, collapsing on the level ground beyond with a rumbling thud that seemed like a small earthquake.

Jason did not wait for the dust to clear. *"Go!"*

Clark's group ran forward to the breached wall and through it to the outside. Namon's group followed close at their heels, with Tano, Jason and Laneena behind them.

They ran. Harder than they thought possible.

Sheer rock walls surrounded the Citadel on three sides of the narrow plateau, and on the fourth side the ground jutted out into open space and then stopped abruptly. Behind them, scores of Epos were running for the pass in the mountain and the trail leading down to the plain below. There was not time for Jason and the others to reach that trail now, nor could they hope for safety among the Epos if they did.

Onward they raced, until at last they could go no farther. They had reached the edge of the cliff, and nothing was ahead of them now except a sheer drop of three hundred meters or more.

Above the sounds of panic and flight the ever increasing roar of the power generators droned on, louder and louder. Finally, knowing his shouted words could not be heard, Jason motioned for them all to drop to the ground and lie flat.

Jason held Laneena close to him, shielding her with his own body, knowing this could well be their last moment together. He wondered how many of the Epos and their human conspirators had escaped the Citadel. He wondered if he would ever know the truth behind the strange machinery, and if—

Thundering power erupted suddenly.

With a roar that seemed to come from deep within the heart of the planet, the Citadel was torn apart. Billowing pressure waves lifted massive stone walls as if they had no weight. A blaze of light lit up the sky with such intensity that even with their faces shielded and their eyes closed, they all were temporarily blinded.

And as the rumbling concussion wave spread outward, great chunks of rock hurtled toward them. . . .

CHAPTER 18

RESCUE FROM AFAR

Masses of rock sprayed out in all directions. Those that did not soar high enough to clear the mountain surrounding three sides of the narrow plateau slid back down the steep slopes and piled in massive heaps at the bottom.

Because the laboratory had been located below ground level in the Citadel, virtually all of the debris arced out on a trajectory that carried it well above the surface of the ground. Those fragments that shot toward the open side of the plateau passed high above the humans and Tano, arcing past the cliff to tumble down to the plain below.

Moments later, it was over.

Swirling clouds of smoke and dust issued from the smoldering pit where once the Citadel had stood. Now nothing remained but the bits of unrecognizable rubble that had dropped back into the depression.

Jason still held Laneena sheltered within his arms, long after the last echoes of tumbling debris had faded. His sight returning now, he looked up and her gaze met his, her gray eyes mirroring his emotions. Another long moment passed before Jason helped her to her feet, gently brushing dust and tiny rock fragments from her hair.

"Are you all right?" he asked.

"I will be when my ears stop ringing."

"Same here."

Once certain she was uninjured, Jason went to check the others. Everyone was stirring now, and Clark and Cosgrove were already moving amongst them, seeing if anyone was hurt. Miraculously, no one was.

Jason stood gazing at the spot where the Citadel had been, and at the mountains behind it. Where the pass had cut through them he could now see only tumbled rock. Hearing Tano's approach, he turned.

"The trail to the plain is blocked by debris," Jason told the steed. "Guards from the city can't get up here, and we can't get down."

Tano twisted his head slightly, as if listening. The decorated collar that was his communications device was undamaged and still functioning.

"Help will arrive shortly," Tano said. "A transport is almost here."

There was nothing to do but wait. He walked back to where Laneena stood and stared out past the edge of the cliff. The only sound now was the wind that played its grim tune in the mountains, now whistling, now moaning, winding and twisting through the cavities of rock. It surged over the weathered surfaces, creating eerie melodies.

"Look," Laneena said suddenly, pointing below.

Distant energy flares were illuminating the city of the Epos in a barrage of flashes. Silhouetted against the intermittent light were dark forms that glided through the air above the city, moving smoothly, surely, and in utter silence. Strange ships with powerful weapons. Open warfare engulfed the city on the plain, but it was a battle that did not last long. Within minutes, all was still again.

Tano looked not at the scene below, but at the sky. Then suddenly his words invaded their minds. *"They are here."*

In the darkness, Jason had not seen the airship approach. Now light beams probed the surface of the narrow plateau, searching, moving, finally pinpointing the spot where the group of people waited. As the silent ship drew nearer, the reflected light of its beams made its form faintly visible.

Oval in shape, the airship had flat upper and lower surfaces, the sides perpendicular to the top and bottom. The smoothly polished surface appeared to be made of some metal alloy. Sixty meters in length and forty-five meters at its widest point, the craft had only a small number of view ports. Their location in a single row suggested there was but one level or deck for passengers in the ship. Something to be expected in an equine technology.

Tano faced the ship, directing telepathic messages to the unseen commander and crew. It took only seconds for the large craft to maneuver close to the edge of the cliff. At a few meters' distance from the rocky precipice the ship halted, holding its position as if rigidly moored there. With the faint sound of servos operating, a wide hatch opened in the side of the ship and a ramp extended to the ground.

Tano said to the humans around him, "We may board now."

Jason and Laneena followed him into the ship without hesitation, and the others were close behind them. Only Oleg Rondell seemed overly cautious about entering the strange craft, but enter it he did, for he was not about to be left behind on that desolate cliff.

Inside, there were three crew members operating the ship. They stood watch over the wide console, directing their simian mind slaves who worked the controls. There was more than enough room for the fifty-one people, although it was obvious they would have to stand, since no seats were utilized by the Epos.

Tano conferred with a small contingent of Epos soldiers who stood garbed in ray armor and other gear, and who bore weapons the earthmen had not seen before. Then after several minutes he left them and approached Jason.

"They are surprised by the Citadel's complete destruction," Tano explained. "They came prepared for a battle."

"What about the city?"

"All of the outcasts have been captured. They could offer little resistance to our forces. Had we known of the oppression your race suffered under the outcasts, we would have sent troops long before this."

"What will happen to them now?"

"That," Tano said, "will have to be decided by our leaders. . . ."

CHAPTER 19

VAULT OF THE GODS

Dromii blazed in the sky overhead, bearing down on the steamy forest with the full warmth of day. A week had passed since the destruction of the Citadel and the complete defeat of the outcast Epos. Those humans that had been enslaved by them were freed, allowed to join either the human settlement to the north or the people of the swamp.

Work on the *Eclipse* was well under way. Epos engineers had brought their own heavy-duty equipment to reposition the ship's massive trans-space engine and repair both it and the power storage cell. Flight Engineer Brant and his technicians worked side by side with the aliens, exchanging technical knowledge and assisting in the restoration of the ship's propulsion system.

But repairs were not the only activity of the day. Something else was taking shape: a joint expedition of humans and Epos to find the source of the mysterious radio signal.

"Everything seems ready, Commander," said First Officer Clark. He stood well out from the ship, near the spot where a small Epos transport was parked. A good forty meters away, in a clearing made just days before, waited one of the full-sized Epos craft. Clark looked in that direction as soldiers from the *Eclipse* joined Epos warriors in boarding the craft. "The men are armed with standard gear, and of course the Epos have their own weapons. Do you really think it will come to a fight?"

"I hope not," said Jason. "We may not even find anything. But we had sure better be prepared."

"You'll get no argument on that, sir. Not after what we've been through so far on this planet." Clark glanced back at the *Eclipse,* where huge sections of the hull had been removed to give access to the engine compartment. "Brant's staying behind to supervise repairs. He thinks we should be through in another six or seven days."

"Good. Once it's done, we'll be ready to go home."

Laneena, standing beside Jason, frowned. "No more than a week?" she said softly, and seemed on the verge of saying something more, but did not.

Jason looked at her and knew what she was thinking. He knew because he had the same troubled thoughts himself. Returning his attention to Clark, he asked, "What about Rondell?"

"Still sulking in his cabin, I suppose," Clark said. "He may never forgive you for going to Trenos without him."

"At the moment, that's the least of my concerns." Jason saw Tano and Lieutenant Cosgrove approaching, coming from the larger Epos craft. "All right. It's time we got started."

Tano bore two of his own tiny "attendants" now, one of them the monkey rescued by Lieutenant Cosgrove in the Citadel. As he reached them the steed nodded in greeting and said telepathically, "The other transport is ready. Your lieutenant has installed one of your Z-wave receivers to enable them to receive the signal as well. Even so, I've directed them to follow us."

"Let's go, then."

Jason and Laneena boarded the small oval craft, followed by Tano, Clark and Cosgrove. Unlike the larger vessel, it was open to the sky with side walls reaching up to the humans' waists, surmounted by a broad railing.

Jason stood at the controls of the Epos' craft. Tano had personally instructed him in its operation, and in a dozen or so flights between the *Eclipse* and the village over the past week, Jason had become expert at it.

"Still locked onto that signal, T.R.?"

"Affirmative, sir," Cosgrove replied.

Jason worked the controls, causing the craft to lift into the air. Then as Cosgrove kept watch on the portable tracking device's indicators, he accelerated forward, quickly reaching cruising velocity.

The larger craft rose behind them, keeping pace with the small transport and maintaining a distance of about a hundred meters. On foot, marching through the dense plant growth, the journey would take days. But moving swiftly through the air they should reach their destination in little more than an hour.

The great expanse of vegetation moved past quickly beneath their craft. Here in the air, they were safe from the beasts of the forest, and their height gave them a new perspective on the terrain and remarkable plant growth.

Even as they neared the mountain range, they could see that the lush, semitropical vegetation extended far up the slopes. Here, at least, there was soil to nurture plant growth, unlike the stark, rocky precipices where the Citadel had been located.

By noon they had reached the base of the mountains. Jason brought the transport to a halt and kept it hovering. To Cosgrove he said, "How are the readings?"

"Strong," the boyish officer replied. "We must be very close."

"Can you pinpoint it?"

"Whatever it is, it's about two hundred meters up the side of the mountain."

Jason adjusted the controls and sent the transport rising along the face of the mountain slope. He was judging the height visually instead of relying on the strangely calibrated instruments of the Epos craft. Plant growth thinned out as they ascended. Much of the slope seemed steep and inaccessible, but as the transport leveled off an area of reasonably smooth, flat ground came into view.

"There's a spot where we can land," Jason told the others. "We'll have to go the rest of the way on foot."

As the craft settled to the ground, Jason switched off the power and disembarked. The others followed.

"Stay close," Jason cautioned them. "If we run into trouble and have to use the energy fields, we can't risk being separated."

They each wore their protective energy shield devices, and Tano was no exception. Since the Epos had nothing similar to them, two of the units had been modified and interconnected, and were fastened upon the steed's woven covering, within easy reach of his attendants.

The large transport was just rising into view behind them. It leveled off even with the ground where the smaller vessel was parked and extended its ramp. But rather than wait for the other soldiers, both Epos and human, to join them, Jason and his group advanced along the face of the mountain.

"We're level with it now," Cosgrove announced as they walked. "But if my readings are correct, then the source of the signal isn't on the surface. It's somewhere deep within the mountain."

"Within?" Clark said, taken aback. "I guess that knocks my crashed-spacecraft theory into a cocked hat!"

The trail turned to the left, following the curve of a massive outcropping of stone. Suddenly, the mouth of a cave came into view. It had not previously been visible, due to the terrain and vegetation. Jason halted the group.

"It must be in there," he said softly. "Have your weapons ready, just in case."

The soldiers from the large transport were still some distance behind them on the trail, brandishing their own weapons. Jason motioned for them, indicating the cave that was still out of their view. Then he turned and led the others inside.

Sunlight reached a considerable distance into the cave. Stretching back at least thirty meters into the interior of the mountain, the shaft ran level and slightly to the left. When the five reached this point, they discovered that it abruptly turned to the right and led off into darkness.

Jason drew a light tube from his equipment pack and flashed the beam about the new shaft. "The natural cave ends here," he said. "Look at the walls ahead: they're straight, and smooth as glass. It's been cut through the rock."

"And fused, from the look of it," said Clark. "As neat a job as I've ever seen."

Without warning, the entire cave was abruptly plunged into darkness. Only where the beam from Jason's light tube fell was there any illumination. It had happened in a split second.

With startled exclamations, the group turned to stare futilely back at the cave entrance, now cloaked in inky blackness. Even as the others fumbled with their own light tubes, Jason swung his around and flashed the beam down the shaft. No matter where he moved the spot of light, the beam met only stone.

"A cave-in?" First Officer Clark ventured.

"Not that fast," Jason said. "And there was no sound."

The others had their beams on now, and together they hurried back down the shaft. It was considerably shorter now—no more than twenty meters to the end. The last ten meters of the shaft now appeared to be solid stone, as if the entrance had never even been there.

Remembering the false wall in the laboratory, Jason said, "Do you suppose it could be an illusion?"

Clark rapped at the stone with the butt of his pistol. "If it is, it's a ruddy *solid* illusion."

"The others are still out there," Laneena said suddenly. "If they didn't see the cave entrance before it vanished, they won't know what happened to us."

"Stand back," Tano's words came into their minds. "I will see if I can cut through."

As the others moved clear, the steed's tiny mind slaves became alert and raised heat ray pistols toward the end of the cave. They fired, the twin beams dazzling in the dim light. For a full minute the beams played across the stone, but utterly without effect.

When the pistols had been put away, Jason carefully felt the stone. "Not even warm," he said. "Something must have blocked the heat, or drawn it off."

Clark asked, "What about trying the force guns?"

"I doubt we'd have any better luck with those," Jason told him. "Besides, in these close quarters, we don't dare use them."

Laneena was standing very still now, her arms folded about her as if she felt a chill. Her head was tilted back as her eyes searched for something she felt lurking just beyond the edge of her senses.

"There's something, or someone, here . . . and not here," she said softly, her words puzzling and oddly disquieting in this place. "I have the feeling they want us here. But they've closed the door behind us."

"Some door," Cosgrove said appreciatively.

"If someone wants us here," Jason said, "then why keep the others out?"

Clark moved warily, his weapon ready. "Perhaps they don't fancy a crowd, Commander."

Jason stepped away from the sealed-off entrance. His senses were alert and he expected at any moment to be confronted by some lurking enemy—perhaps the strange creature he had glimpsed in the Citadel's laboratory. But as the seconds and then the minutes wore on, no new threat came, nothing that smacked of danger. There was only the darkness and the smothering silence.

"All right," Jason said finally, "they've only blocked off the entrance. We may as well see what lies in the other direction."

"May as well," Clark agreed. "Anyone powerful enough to make stone walls materialize out of thin air could kill us here and now if they had a mind to."

They made their way back down the shaft, soon reaching the bend at the end where the cave angled off into a highly polished tunnel. The moving oval pools of brightness from their light tubes lent an eerie look to the strange corridor, and their footfalls echoed from the smooth walls. There was no debris or even dust here in the tunnel, and the air was cool and remarkably dry.

The shaft continued in the same direction for twenty meters, then sharply turned to the left. Jason peered cautiously around the corner, then motioned for the others to follow. In this new direction, roughly parallel with the natural cave, the tunnel reached thirty meters deeper into the mountain. The tunnel abruptly terminated at this point.

A large doorway, taller and wider than conventional human

standards, stood in the left wall of the tunnel, doorless and open. Beyond it was a pitch-black chamber of uncertain dimensions.

Jason moved to the entrance and flashed his beam around the room. It seemed empty, but then if there was one thing he had learned on this world, it was that things were not always as they seemed. Staying close together, the five entered the chamber.

The doorway proved to be in the center of the east wall of a chamber roughly thirty meters square. Apparently the huge room had been cut from the hard stone of the mountain in the same manner as the tunnel. The walls had the same glassy smoothness that made them shiny and appear almost translucent. Yet there was one striking difference between these walls and those of the tunnel.

Stretching completely around the chamber at a point just above their heads, a wide band of decorative carvings had been etched into the stone. Reaching up to a height of two meters, the band was made up of unusual symbols, some of which Jason thought he recognized from the colossal buildings in the city on the plain. So whoever was responsible for that ancient city had likely built this remarkable vault.

By chance, Jason directed his light beam upward to the ceiling. The chamber was quite high. Then, as his beam pointed almost straight up, Jason suddenly froze.

In the next moment, they were all looking up toward the ceiling, staring in astonishment at the thing above them. . . .

CHAPTER 20

MEETING WITH THE KORLON

"What is it?" Cosgrove said, his voice echoing faintly from the distant walls.

The five began backing away from the center of the room. Above them, revealed in the glow of their combined light beams, a large object was suspended in the air. Nine meters tall and three wide, the thing had the shape of an elongated pyramid with the pointed end down. Its corners and edges were smoothly rounded, and it seemed solidly cast of some substance which might be metallic, and yet which was subtly unlike any familiar metal.

No tangible support held the strange object in the air, yet it seemed locked in place, still and unmoving. Floating in the exact center of the chamber, it seemed somehow removed from the laws of physics that should be acting upon it.

"What's your scanner doing?" Jason asked the young lieutenant.

"It's completely jammed," Cosgrove answered. "That thing must be the source of the signal. But what's the purpose of it?"

"Apparently," said Jason, "to bring *us* here. That city the outcast Epos had taken over—it was built by an older culture. We know that much at least. But I didn't realize they were advanced enough to produce something like this."

"But what happened to them?" Clark said. "A race that advanced wouldn't just die out without leaving traces of their culture and technology behind in the city. There was nothing there but the buildings."

"Who says they died out? Maybe they just packed up and moved on."

Clark considered the possibilities. "And you think this thing is their way of leaving a forwarding address?"

Jason gave a short, hard laugh. Then he studied the floating object with new regard. "I wonder."

Laneena had been staring at the object continuously since first seeing it. Her expression was strange, as if she already sensed something fantastic about the device.

"They're here," she said softly. "The ones who watch. Here . . . and yet not here. There's an intelligence within the thing, Jason. A mind unlike any I've ever touched."

Tano too was alert and receptive to the device. "Yes, a mind. I sense it is a monitor of some sort. It reminds me of some of our telepathic locking devices, only it is infinitely more complicated."

As Laneena concentrated on the floating object she began to feel as if she were penetrating its outer shell and reaching through to the inside. What's more, she became aware of Tano's mental presence. She felt their minds touch within the mysterious alien device. She had heard the "silent voices" of Epos minds before, yet this was different. For the device above them seemed to amplify their contact, and it was not Tano's words she perceived now, but the essence of his spirit. Much of that mind felt familiar, yet much was oddly alien. It was an orderly mind, scientific and well disciplined on the surface, but whose ruling passions were boldness, zeal and a bit of impetuosity. It was a curiously masculine mind, intense and mildly intimidating.

The mind of the alien device itself was another matter. Laneena sensed it was a manufactured intelligence, cool and impartial. Utterly direct and without guile. Yet it was so complex and enormous she felt lost in its convolutions. Tano seemed to be exploring it methodically, searching for something that would enable him to understand it. The key that would unlock its mystery. She tried to stay with him, to maintain that fragile contact, and realized suddenly that the effort to probe the device was sapping her mental strength. Already, her ties with the real world around her was growing faint and confused. The chamber seemed to swirl about her as her mind fell into the enormous depth of the intellect before her.

Laneena—

The word touched her, and she recognized it as her name. But she was not sure whether it had come from her own mind or from some corner of the vast alien intelligence.

Laneena! came the word again, and this time it reached out to her, like a rope thrown to someone caught in the turbulent waters of a river. Gradually, she began to pull away from the mental currents that surged and eddied around her. The room came back to its proper perspective, and Laneena became aware that she was looking into Jason's concerned gaze. He was standing directly before her now, and with a sigh she relaxed into his firm arms.

"Are you all right?" he asked.

"Yes . . . but that thing . . ."

Abruptly, something began to change within the chamber. Before, their light tubes had cast only a minor glow about the enormous room. But that glow was augmented by light of a different nature—light that seemed to have no source.

The walls steadily became more brightly illuminated, until the chamber's interior was almost as bright as day. Jason was just considering the advisability of leaving when he noticed that the door through which they had entered was no longer there. The wall where it had been was completely solid.

Tano himself was shaking free of the device's mind now, and was looking about the surprisingly bright chamber in bewilderment.

"Something must have been triggered," Jason said. "I'm not sure our weapons will work against any of this, but if we have to use them—"

Before he could finish speaking, a voice came from the strange object which floated above them.

"Your weapons cannot be used against us," the voice told them. Its tone was majestic, melodic, though vaguely nonhuman. Yet it did not warn or threaten, or even scold. It merely informed. "There is no need for weapons. Do not fear us."

At the same time, the floating object itself was undergoing changes. On the lower surfaces of the elongated and inverted pyramid, images were forming. Or rather, the same image, repeated upon each of the device's four sides.

The colors were vivid and the image real and three-dimensional. As it cleared, a face looked down at them. It was humanoid in form, but distinctly different from any humans Jason had ever encountered. It was a face totally without malice or evil intent. It seemed to inspire confidence and a feeling of well-being. But were these feelings to be trusted? One thing, at least: it was not the ghastly face of the creature they had glimpsed in the Epos' secret laboratory.

"Please stay back," the voice said.

Instantly, a beam of energy spread down from the bottom of the object. It struck in the center of the chamber floor, where it dispersed to form a circle nearly seven meters wide. Then within the circle, another object formed. The radiant energy seemed to mold itself, to flow into the shape of a circular platform. At the center of the platform was a small energy globe half a meter in diameter, pulsing with an eerie light.

"It is complete," the voice said. "Please stand upon the transport vehicle."

They hesitated.

Jason asked, "Do we have a choice?"

There was a pause, then Jason saw that the door was again present in the wall. The voice from the floating object said, "You may leave if you wish. But please, do as we say. You will not be harmed."

Jason studied the face that loomed above them, godlike and beneficent. The creature could be lying, he supposed, yet he had a gut feeling he could trust in those words.

Turning to the others, he said, "I won't order anyone to go, *or* stay. This is something we all have to agree on."

After a moment, Tano said, "We came here to investigate. If we turn back now, we will leave with more questions than answers."

"I agree," Clark said. "Speaking for myself, the gain could well outweigh the risk."

Lieutenant Cosgrove swallowed hard, but nodded affirmatively. "I'm game too, sir."

That left only Laneena's decision, and Jason turned to the girl he still sheltered with one protective arm. She was staring at the face on the alien device with a look of utter fascination, and as she became aware of Jason's attention her eyes swung around to meet his. Excitement seemed to crackle through her trim form, and although there was still a trace of apprehension showing on her features, it was clear that the events of the past few weeks had given her a taste for adventure.

"If you're staying," she told Jason, "then so am I."

"All right," said Jason. "Then it's unanimous. We'll give it a try."

The alien looking down at them gave a smile of approval, like a teacher whose students had just responded with the correct answer to an important question. "We await you, then."

Jason and Laneena stepped up onto the disk-shaped platform. Clark and Cosgrove were right behind them, and Tano soon boarded as well, taking up a position on the other side of the glowing, pulsing energy globe. They did not know what to expect next. The alien had called the platform a "transport," but what manner of transportation was it?

They did not have long to wait for the answer.

The energy globe on the platform pulsed brighter and more rapidly. At the same time, a high-pitched staccato bleeping note began to reverberate through the great chamber, steadily increasing in speed and intensity. A deep, droning note joined it, also ascending, also growing louder.

Then suddenly, the chamber around them began to fade, dissolving into misty gloom. The darkness became the infinite blackness of space, and the spinning globe of Cerus Major fell away behind them. The slight sheen of an energy shell could be seen all around them, enclosing them in a transparent hollow sphere.

Abruptly, even the vast panorama of space began to fade, seeming to fold in upon itself, with the familiar stars winking out of existence. And in an instant's burst of dazzling light, the universe they had known was left behind. For now their unorthodox vehicle was hurtling through the vast expanse of an enormous tunnel. A tunnel that glowed with violet light, pulsing and coruscating with a hazy, dreamlike quality.

Jason had heard theories before about the possibility of gateways to other universes, but they had been only theories. Even the recent development of hyperspace drive had not led to the discovery of new and unknown dimensions.

Something lay ahead of them. Coming into view was a bright and glowing field of energy that seemed to be the other end of the tunnel. Their vehicle hurtled onward, through the oscillating field and into space.

But it was an alien space, bizarre and totally unfamiliar.

It was not the inky black void of Jason's universe. Light was everywhere, a golden light that seemed to filter throughout the incredibly vast expanse of space, yet without issuing from any star. There were no stars here, no glowing points of light. There were only countless specks of matter—black bodies, large and small. Planets perhaps . . . or something else.

In the distance, if distance could even be conceived of in this strange realm, was something that could not be compared with anything in the known universe. Larger than a star, perhaps larger than a galaxy, a great globe twinkled with energies, glowing like illuminated crystal, animated and twinkling. Its interior was in a state of flux, seemingly solid and yet beyond all concepts of solid matter, and Jason found that looking into its depths produced an almost hypnotic effect.

Still moving unbelievably fast, their vehicle was now on a course that would take it straight to one of the larger black bodies. Abruptly, a voice issued from their craft once more.

"The changeover is complete. You are now in an aggregate galactic system that we call ectocosmic space. Your destination is the planet Zero Tau-Alpha. You will find its gravity and atmosphere compatible."

Jason was still fascinated with the magnificent glowing orb to their right. "Please," he said, "tell me what that starlike object is."

"The Chronos-Sphere," replied the disembodied voice. "It is the heart of this universe, and indeed of all existence."

As the vehicle moved deeper into the planet's layers of atmosphere, they could see that despite its previous appearance of total darkness, it was a planet that in many ways resembled Earth or Cerus Major. Only the bright glow of space had made it a silhouette. Under a sky slightly more emerald than blue, great mountain ranges could be seen, as well as forests and plains. Similar, but subtly different. Odd and weirdly beautiful.

Slowing now, their craft descended to a wide plain that stretched smooth and flat for hundreds of kilometers in all directions. An object stood in the center of the plain, an object that seemed small at first, but which soon loomed large as the distance between it and the approaching craft decreased.

The immense cube was several kilometers wide, high and deep. It hovered rigidly perhaps thirty meters above the surface of the plain. No markings covered the sides of the cube, which had the gentle sheen of brushed copper.

Clark stared in amazement at the fantastically large cube. "What do you make of that, Commander? Is it a city . . . or some kind of gigantic spacecraft?"

"I don't know," said Jason. "Perhaps both."

Their vehicle was now less than forty meters from the enormous cube. The craft slowed and settled gently to the ground. Its energy shield dropped away, and as it did a soft breeze swept over them. An alien breeze, it held the scent of distant exotic plants and things unknown.

Jason and the others cautiously left the disk-shaped platform and tested the ground. The sandy soil was firm beneath their feet. Its color was almost pure crystalline white, and seemed free of other kinds of soil or rocks. The entire plain reminded Jason of an ancient sea bottom, the water evaporated to leave only a thick crust of salt, dry and bleached.

At once, a beam of light flashed down from the center of the side of the cube facing them. It projected a pattern on the sand, in the form of a red and white grid.

"We are to stand there," Laneena said softly.

Jason looked at her oddly. "How do you know?"

"I just . . . know."

Trusting to the young woman's remarkable mental acuity, the humans and the Epos soldier stepped onto the projected pattern of light. As soon as they were all in place, the beam began to shimmer. The scene around them faded, blurred into mist, and was replaced by the interior of some great room. A teleporter station, no doubt. But whatever walls or ceiling there might be could not be seen, as they were hidden in darkness. Yet the room was not dark, for Jason and the others were brightly illuminated.

Before they had a chance to wander from the area, a voice called out to them. A new voice, soft and mellow. *Follow,* it said. Its source was a hovering ball of light that had suddenly materialized nearby. Elongating slightly, it moved off, leaving a wispy trail of fading light in its wake.

Follow, it said again. And so they followed.

Unusual objects of crystal and metal reached high into the air around them, and were so totally alien in design that it was impossible to tell whether they were functional devices or merely decorations conceived by nonhuman minds. Jason could not clearly see a ceiling overhead, but sensed there was one not far above the tops of the strange objects around them. He imagined that this mammoth cube could easily contain a hundred or more levels. Where they were within the complex was anybody's guess.

Ahead of them now were massive crystalline chambers that almost certainly were power generators, perhaps the ones that energized the teleporter. No one was present to operate the equipment. It had to have been controlled from another location.

The guide now turned abruptly to the right, leading them to a freestanding portal that was glowing emerald green. Through the portal could be seen nothing but darkness, and again, it seemed more a decorative touch. For if there were no walls, of what use were doors?

The answer came as Jason and the others passed through the shimmering frame. At once, the view behind them faded. Ahead, a different area was now visible. They could still see the portal itself, but they were obviously in a completely different part of the complex.

Here was an abundance of lights and forms, still within a dark, limbolike realm, but of such dazzling beauty and color that the objects in the first section of the complex took their proper place as mere functional mechanisms. Here were fountains, splashing and spraying, but with *light* instead of water. Crystalline forms suspended in the air slowly revolved, scattering pleasing reflections everywhere.

And here also were the aliens.

They were tall, at least three meters high, as Jason had guessed from the scale of the buildings in the ancient city. And they were humanoid. Their heads were slightly larger in proportion to their bodies than Earth's humans, and their features were more widely set.

Dressed in full-length, billowing robes that sparkled and shone with unnatural light, their very appearance spoke of wisdom, and of knowledge so vast as to humble the petty technology of Earth. Their skin tone was mostly red with tracings of blue, and looking at them gave the odd impression of gazing at a negative image. Golden eyes that almost glowed looked kindly at them, and warm smiles beamed down.

The alien nearest them spoke first, nearly bubbling with enthusiasm. *"Welcome,"* he said. "This is truly a day of monumental significance! You are the first, of all the worlds chosen. The fruit of a seed planted so very long ago. We—"

"Klon," the other alien said reprovingly, "you are getting ahead of yourself. Our guests deserve a proper explanation." Turning to Jason and the others, he said, "We are the Korlon. By your standards, we are a most ancient race. I am called Shom; this is my friend Klon."

"I would introduce ourselves," said Jason, "but I have a feeling you already know who we are."

Shom smiled enigmatically. "As you may have guessed, we developed as a race on the planet you call Cerus Major. For countless eons it was our home. From time to time, we still monitor the happenings on the planet's surface."

Clark said, "How long have you been here?"

"For approximately one thousand Earth years," Shom answered. "The discovery that permitted us to enter this space system was fairly recent in our history. It was not possible until our advancement to a twelfth-order science."

"Twelfth-order?"

"Merely a technical designation. Your own world has just reached a fifth-order science, and yours"—he turned to Tano—"is on the verge of fifth-order. Perhaps another year or so."

Jason tried to imagine the technological gap involved. It was impossible.

Klon now spoke again. "About one hundred million years ago, Korlon emissaries were sent throughout your galaxy. On planets which had developed cultures, our presence was never known. But on those worlds without civilizations, we selected individuals of the most promising species. These individuals were trained to lead their fellow creatures, and given knowledge. And so the seeds were sown . . . on Earth, on the Epos' first world of Tabree, and others. Many others. Once started, these cultures were allowed to develop on their own, and we waited these many years for the first contact."

"Then," Clark said, "you claim responsibility for our development?"

"No—not totally. We were only a factor, and there were many other factors, some far more important than our own influence."

"You brought us to Cerus Major, didn't you?" Jason said suddenly. "Deflected our course while in space leap so we would have to land there."

Shom answered the question. "Yes, we did. It was an unforgivable act of intrusion, I confess. Such manipulation was not originally part of our plan. In other cases, such as with your ancestors"—he nodded toward Laneena and Tano—"we brought ships to our ancient homeworld because their survival depended upon it. They would have perished needlessly otherwise. And so we chose to let them develop on Cerus Major. In your case," Shom told Jason, "other matters prompted us to bring you there, in the hope you would find our beacon, and prove to be the type of being we were seeking."

For whatever respect Jason had for the aliens' technology, there was still bitterness in his voice as he said, "That manipulation cost one of my men his life, and jeopardized the lives and safety of the rest of us."

Shom's features sagged into a look of such sadness that its sincerity could not be questioned. "We deeply regret that," he said. "It was never our intent that anyone should suffer from our actions, nor do we hold your lives in such little regard as to endanger them for a mere whim. But beyond the simple act of deflecting ships to our ancient homeworld, we are bound by laws of our own making, formulated centuries ago, that prevent us from interfering in the events which take place on Cerus Major and all other worlds. Only in one highly special case of outside interference may we intervene. That may seem heartless or even cruel to you under the circumstances. But please understand that the enormous responsibility of our knowledge and power forced us to create those rules. And to ensure that we abide by them, certain automatic and irrevocable safeguards were created. To depart from the limits we have set for ourselves would be to forfeit everything—even our existence. Otherwise, we would certainly have done everything we could to safeguard your lives, and to prevent the unjust enslavement of humans by the outcast Epos."

"Maybe we can accept that," Tano commented. "But we saw a creature on the planet, with greatly advanced technology, who had no qualms about interfering in events there."

"Yes," Klon spoke. "We know. They are in many ways like ourselves, possessing a twelfth-order technology and having crossed the barriers to ectocosmic space." There was a mixture of loathing and regret in Klon's words. "In every other respect, they are the antithesis of our race."

"Who are they?" Jason asked.

"The Jorils. Their race developed on our sister world, Cerus Minor. But they know nothing of compassion or goodness. Since they were first able to travel to other worlds, they have tried to enslave or control every race of beings they met, in your galaxy and others. Only by our efforts over the centuries have we prevented their seizing your own solar system and its neighboring systems. We are their nemesis, and they ours."

"The exception to the rule?" Jason said speculatively. "The outside interference you *are* allowed to thwart?"

"Exactly," Klon replied. "Because their power rivals ours."

Shom looked especially concerned. "We learned of the Jorils' involvement with the outcast Epos no sooner than you did. Normally, the energy levels of their devices can be detected by our probes, alerting us to their presence. In this case, they were either using their most minor equipment, or . . ."

Klon finished the statement for him. "Or they have finally succeeded in improving their shielding techniques. Exactly as we have feared."

"You diverted us here," Jason said suddenly, "knowing that we'd get involved and help free the people from the outcast Epos. You used us to accomplish what you yourselves were not allowed to do, didn't you? Our space-leap technology just made it far easier for you to get us here quickly and unobtrusively."

Shom only smiled and continued. "For thousands of years our

power and that of the Jorils have been evenly matched. We fear that may be changing, for the worse. There is reason to believe the Jorils are readying a new offensive, and have developed techniques which we have not yet found ways to counter. There is no doubt we *can* counter them, given enough time, but one of our greatest weaknesses is that while the Jorils are physically free to go anywhere in the cosmos, we on the other hand are restricted by our nature to this complex. True, we do have remote sensors, automated probes and other devices to do much of our work, but it would be so much easier for beings like yourselves to go where we cannot go, and do what we cannot do."

"What Shom tells you is correct," Klon said. "You see, you have not yet lost the abilities we once had, ages ago. Your ways are more direct, more . . . if you will forgive the term, *barbaric*. With your methods, and the training and equipment we can furnish, you *could* be of enormous help in our continuing efforts against the Jorilian Empire."

"Perhaps," Jason said, "but for now, I still have a ship to return to Earth, along with the people entrusted to me."

There was a moment of silence during which the two Korlon exchanged glances, then nodded. Finally, Shom spoke. "Your responsibility is understood and appreciated. We approve of your decision."

Shom now turned to a low crystal table to his left. As he gazed into its center, a pattern of colored lights began to blaze and whirl within the depths of the transparent material. In seconds, a small object had materialized atop the table. A red-hued disk, eight centimeters in diameter and three centimeters thick, it had no visible circuitry or devices within its transparent depths. But then, neither had the table which produced it.

Shom picked the disk up and held it out to Jason. It seemed small in the large, gloved hand of the Korlon. Stepping forward, Jason accepted the disk.

"Keep this with you," Shom explained. "With it, you will be able to contact us if you wish."

Jason was still looking into the ruby depths of the disk. "What of the others we left back at the cave?"

"We must insist they know nothing of this. We do not wish to make our existence known in your galaxy. Your worlds are not yet ready for full contact with us."

Jason looked up at them. "As you wish, then."

Klon said, "If you will return to the transport now, we will return you to Cerus Major and your friends. We wish you luck, and will be monitoring your progress there."

Shom gestured toward the portal. "You will be led back to the entrance chamber."

The glowing orb that had guided them to the aliens now reappeared near the portal. It seemed to beckon to them, directing them to follow. Jason pocketed the ruby disk, and as he neared the portal, he looked again upon the faces of the two Korlon. He still had not made up his mind about these remarkable aliens, but for the moment he had more pressing matters to consider.

The return to the transport was quick and without event. No sooner had they all stepped onto the disk-shaped platform than it began to rise swiftly into the air, again without the slightest sensation of movement. It soared rapidly into space, its sphere of protective energy again encircling all.

Soon, the golden realm of ectocosmic space was left behind as the transport hurtled back through the great pulsating tunnel that bridged the two space systems. The amazing vehicle reappeared in galactic space, plunging back toward the atmosphere of Cerus Major.

Moments later, the stone walls of the great chamber seemed to reform around them. They were once more within the mountain vault, and as their senses cleared and they stepped down from the platform, the odd vehicle vanished from sight. All was as it was before. The pyramid-shaped object still floated rigidly, timelessly, above them.

Laneena's eyes were moist, her look dazzled, as she spoke to Jason. "It was all so incredible . . . so . . . *impossible*. Do you think they told the truth? Was it all real, or just some fantastic illusion? I'm not sure I can tell the difference anymore."

Jason looked into the depths of the red disk he had taken from his pocket. It seemed to twinkle with an amused energy of its own.

"I think we can believe them," he said. "I think we *have* to." Putting the disk away once more, he added, "Now let's get back to the others. And remember to watch what you say."

As they reached the end of the cave they found the entrance was open again. The barrier had been removed. Emerging into the daylight and warm air, they could see the other earthmen and Epos soldiers well beyond the cave entrance, spread out in a wide pattern, combing the side of the mountain.

Jason called out to them. "Over here!"

At once the others turned at the sound of his voice and started back. The first to reach Jason and the others was a crew member of the *Eclipse*. His tone was apologetic and puzzled as he said, "What happened, sir? We lost track of you."

"Sorry," Jason told him. "We were . . . checking out that cave."

The crewman looked in the direction he indicated, and as his eyes took in the cave entrance, his puzzled look became one of complete bafflement. "I don't understand. We had to go past that area at least two or three times. I'd *swear* there was no cave there."

"You were looking for us," Jason said. "You probably didn't notice."

On impulse, the crewman started toward the cave entrance. Jason moved to intercept him.

"There's nothing there," he told the man, regretful that he had to lie to him.

The crewman peered inside anyway, his eyes striving to make out details in the gloomy interior. "Yeah," he said, "not much to look at, is it?"

Surprised, Jason looked in as well. The cave that had stretched back thirty meters before turning into the polished tunnel leading to the vault now ended in less than twenty meters. Its rear wall bore no openings at all.

"Well," said the crewman, turning away from the entrance and shaking his head, "I still don't see how we missed it. But there's no denying it's there."

"Commander—" Lieutenant Cosgrove said suddenly. "The signal . . . it's stopped."

Jason looked at the tracking scanner Cosgrove held. It was true. The mysterious signal that had brought them here was now silent. Its purpose was fulfilled.

The crewman said, "What do we do now, Commander?"

"We may as well head back," Jason told him. "We're not going to find anything around here."

As the rest of them regrouped and made their way back toward the ships, Jason spoke with Tano. "What will you tell your superiors?"

The Epos steed replied, "That we found no trace of any creatures like the one we saw in the laboratory. That much is the truth at any rate. Beyond that, I think they will accept the idea that the signal was merely some natural phenomenon. Or perhaps a malfunction of your equipment. We never *did* receive it on ours."

Jason sensed a trace of humor in Tano's thoughts, and it was a characteristic he had not noticed before. Perhaps the steed felt enough of a sense of comradeship with them now to joke.

As they reached the area of the ships, Jason held back a short distance and gently pulled Laneena to a halt beside him. "We have to speak," he said as the others continued on out of earshot.

She searched his eyes, sensing something important lay behind his action. "Yes?"

"There's still something we haven't settled," he told her, his voice becoming tender and a bit hesitant. "Something that I *want* to settle, once and for all, before we head back."

Her expression was cautious. "Go on."

Jason took a deep breath and let it out. "I've no right to ask you to go against your father's wishes, or the ways of your people, but I can't keep silent any longer. I love you, Laneena . . . more than anything else in this universe, or any *other* universe. And if you do care for me—"

"If I care for you?" she said abruptly, incredulously. Sounding suddenly like her father, she said, "It's a blind fool you are, Jason Smith, if you don't know I do."

And with that she reached out and seized the wide bands of his webbing harness, pulling him firmly toward her. Her lips burned against his in the next moment, and for several long moments thereafter. When at last she backed away a bit, breathless and amused by her own boldness, her mist-gray eyes fixed him with a look both tender and fiery.

"After all we've been through," she told him with absolute conviction, "I'm not going to give you up without a fight!"

CHAPTER 21

NEW BEGINNINGS

"You dare to ask me to forsake our traditions?" Shannon thundered in the meeting hall of the village government building, beneath the great dome of the city-plant. "You want me to cast our traditions aside, like last week's refuse, just because they do not please you? Disregard my own feelings if you will, girl, but what of our people? Do they not deserve better treatment than to have their expectations crushed?"

Laneena looked shattered by her father's obstinacy. She had expected a bad reaction to her request to be excused from the traditions which bound her selection of a marriage partner, but Shannon had exploded without even giving her a chance to explain why. She flashed a troubled look at Jason as he stood by her, his hand grasping hers.

"I—I'm sorry you feel that way, Father," she said. "I truly am. But you *must* try to consider *my* feelings, too."

Shannon came forward, placing his large hands upon her slender shoulders. "Of course I do, Daughter," he said, his tone more gentle now, but still rock-firm. "You're a darlin' child, and the light of my life. I want only the best for you. But the tradition which says you must marry the very best man in our village is an important one. Doubly so, since I have no son, and 'twill be no more Shannons guiding our village. I'm sorry, Laneena, but the tradition must stand."

"That's your final word?" Laneena asked. "You will insist that I marry Namon?" Her gaze darted to where the young village warrior stood on the opposite side of the table, Roanne at his side. The couple looked as downcast as she felt.

"Namon?" Shannon said, as if hearing that name for the first time. "Namon? Well, now, girl, you've got me puzzled, indeed. True it is that Namon has always been considered the strongest and bravest of our young village men. But although he's a fine lad and I don't wish to take anything from him," Shannon continued, his look of innocence suddenly giving way to an impish grin, "still, I'd have to say that after what's happened in the past few weeks, the very *best* man in this village is the one standing there next to you."

It took only a heartbeat for her to realize that he meant Jason, and that he had been teasing her from the start. With a great sigh of relief and joy, she embraced Shannon.

"Oh, Father—how long have you known?"

"Well now," he said, "not as long as I should have, considering the evidence was right there in front of me. But long enough, darlin'. Long enough."

Laneena kissed his cheek, then pulled back away. "But . . . you realize I'll want to go with Jason. Not that I want to leave here, but—"

"We'll not talk of leavings now," Shannon told her, his eyes not sharing the smile his lips still formed. He brushed a strand of hair away from her moistening eyes. "There'll be time enough for that later. As for now, it had better be marriage you're planning with this young man here, for the villagers have their hearts set on a big wedding."

Shannon reached out and grasped the hand Jason offered in friendship and thanks. Then as he cocked an eye back toward the other couple in the meeting room, his impish look returned.

"Just a minute, now," he said. "It seems all's not right here! We've promised Namon a bride, and it's hardly fair we go back on our word. I don't suppose anybody might have a suggestion?"

Roanne smiled, all the worry and frustration gone from her lovely features. "I have an idea," she said.

"As I thought you might!" Shannon gave a hearty chuckle, and with brawny arms reached out to embrace them all. . . .